Praise for Luis Alberto Urrea's
The Water Museum

ONE OF THE BEST BOOKS OF THE YEAR

Washington Post, National Public Radio, Men's Journal,
Kirkus Reviews

"All thirteen stories are realistic and unsparing, as un-flinching and hard-hitting as they are beautiful. It's difficult to find comparisons to an author as original as Urrea, a kind of literary badass who still believes in love. *The Water Museum* is a brilliant, powerful collection, and Luis Alberto Urrea is a master storyteller with a rock and roll heart."   —Alan Cheuse, National Public Radio

"Magic.... Urrea skillfully evokes the semi-comic experi-ence of the sensitive observer who is both part of and outside of a community."

—Michael Lindgren, *Washington Post*

"Like Urrea, we care deeply for his characters. He writes with compassion and humor and with a nod to the creep-ing darkness within us all."

—Natalie Serber, *The Oregonian*

"Urrea has a gift for replicating street slang and outfitting his urban landscapes with graffiti, freeway grids, and people of all races....His thirteen pulsing yarns are intense and fast-paced."   —Don Waters, *San Francisco Chronicle*

"One of the most prolific bicultural and bilingual writers today....These stories will leave you breathless....There's something universal and timeless about them."
    —Liliana Valenzuela, *Austin American–Statesman*

"A consummate craftsman....Nowhere is this American Book Award winner's genre-jumping talent more visible than in his latest collection of short stories....Incredibly moving....For a collection that traipses themes of doomed relationships, identity, religious awe, and social responsibility, *The Water Museum* is refreshingly bereft of a preachy tone and relies upon a kind of folksy power."
    —Roberto Ontiveros, *Dallas Morning News*

"*The Water Museum* mines the tragedy, the dark comedy, and the ultimate futility of erecting walls between cultures....Urrea is a deft, witty observer."
    —Tricia Springstubb, *Cleveland Plain Dealer*

"Pitch-perfect and penetrating, *The Water Museum* traverses the rich borderlands of the human heart with humor, mystery, and grit."   —Amy Jo Burns, *Ploughshares*

The Water Museum

Also by Luis Alberto Urrea

FICTION

Queen of America

Into the Beautiful North

The Hummingbird's Daughter

In Search of Snow

Six Kinds of Sky

Mr. Mendoza's Paintbrush (graphic novel; artwork by
Christopher Cardinale)

NONFICTION

The Devil's Highway: A True Story

Across the Wire: Life and Hard Times on the Mexican Border

*By the Lake of Sleeping Children: The Secret Life of the
Mexican Border*

Nobody's Son

Wandering Time

POETRY

The Tijuana Book of the Dead

The Fever of Being

Ghost Sickness

Vatos

The Water Museum

Stories

Luis Alberto Urrea

BACK BAY BOOKS
Little, Brown and Company
New York Boston London

Back Bay Books / Little, Brown and Company
Hachette Book Group
1290 Avenue of the Americas, New York, NY 10104
littlebrown.com

Originally published in hardcover by Little, Brown and Company, April 2015

First Back Bay trade paperback edition, April 2016

Back Bay Books is an imprint of Little, Brown and Company, a division of Hachette Book Group, Inc. The Back Bay Books name and logo are trademarks of Hachette Book Group, Inc.

The publisher is not responsible for websites (or their content) that are not owned by the publisher.

The Hachette Speakers Bureau provides a wide range of authors for speaking events. To find out more, go to hachettespeakersbureau.com or call (866) 376-6591.

Design by Marie Mundaca

ISBN 978-0-316-33437-2 (hc) / 978-0-316-33439-6 (pb)

LCCN 2014958990

10 9 8 7 6 5 4 3 2

LSC-C

Printed in the United States of America

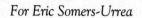
For Eric Somers-Urrea

Man was made at the end of the week's work, when God was tired.

—Mark Twain

Contents

CONTENTS

One

Mountains Without Number

In a beat-down house at the foot of a western butte, a woman sips her coffee and stares at her high school yearbook. Most everybody's gone. The pictures seem to be a day old to her. She still laughs at the drama club portrait, still remembers the shouting when the football team won the regional. And there she is on page thirty. She was one of the pretty ones, for sure. One of the slender ones who had a mouth that suggested to every boy that she knew a secret and was slightly amused by it. She had famous lips.

She looks at herself in her drill team uniform. Runs her finger down her skinny leg. Wonders where that girl went.

Now she keeps the shades at the back of the house pulled down so she doesn't have to look at the cliffs. A few years back a woodpecker got into her roof beam, and it's all chipped out. Wood bees are rooting around in there. She has been meaning to hammer some sheet metal over that corner, but she hasn't seen woodpeckers in years—not since the drouth got ahold of the land. She keeps her geraniums and little apple tree out front alive with her dirty dishwater. Saves money, though her neighbor says that makes her a Democrat. Being eco-logical and all that happy crappy. They laugh about it over the fence some mornings.

"Them apples," the neighbor says, "are gonna come up tastin' like Lemon Joy."

But the old lady isn't out today, and the woman wonders as she often does if the neighbor is dead in there. Some days are spooky like that, and she doesn't know why. She wants everything to live forever.

Her coffee dregs go down the drain, and she rinses the cup in her plastic water bin and upends it in the dish rack and slides her keys off the counter and goes out. Turns hard left out the door so her back is to the butte. She drives a Ford F-150 with 120,000 miles on it. One bumper sticker: HONK TWICE IF YOU'RE ELVIS, with a little yellow smiley face. Backs out and doesn't look up. She can never find Bon Jovi on the radio. Just Jesus and Trace Adkins. But Trace is good enough. The sky feels like it's on fire as she drives into town. Her morning clients are always there before she is. Waiting for her. Feels like the last six people left in the West.

*

Atop the butte, the spirits of the old ones are indistinguishable from the wind. From up there, the old main street is

thinned by altitude and turns silver in the morning sunlight. Crows skitter across the streak of light like small
embers. And her truck pulls into a diagonal slot outlined
in faded yellow paint. The pickup could be any color, any
color at all. It doesn't matter. The sun is turning it gray.
She looks as small as a pebble in a creek bed.

Up there, the wind is an oven, and nobody below knows
there are ancient fire rings and small middens of deer bones
and remnants of lodges where pack rats still gather twigs
from the dead white trees. Scattered across the brow of the
butte, hide scrapers and arrowheads and metates hollowed
out in flat rocks where acorns and pine nuts were ground
by ten thousand years of women smaller than the one below but with the same thick braid of hair. Gray, everywhere
gray, threading its way among the colors, as it has stitched
the fields to the south. Dead watercourses form scars across
the belly of the world. The oaks and the pines are as pale
and colorless now as photographic negatives, except for the
wide black plains to the east: dead oceans of boiling rock.

The few tourists who speed through town on that main
drag don't use film anymore. Their children may never
know what negatives are. If anyone takes a snapshot, it is
on a smartphone. And it will be a picture of these red and
black cliffs, not the town, not the woman.

The colored figures painted upon the face of the butte
are the only relief for a hundred miles: white, blue, yellow.

They call her Frankie. Has been Frankie since high school. It was so cute then, so saucy. Better than Francine, by God.

Frankie pulls herself out of the Ford, wonders how her hip got so stiff. She couldn't ride a horse today if you paid her. Wonders how she got to this time in life when she tries to get up from a booth inside her diner and her hip locks on her and keeps her trapped for an extra minute until her body releases with a click like a door unlocking. How she got to this season of night fevers and wet sheets and spooky moods. Her keys are clipped onto a great purple carabiner with a small foxtail with Indian beads dangling. She sounds like bells as she moves.

Her clients await her in the scant wedge of blue shade along the wall. She nods to her breakfast club and slams the truck door and hates the way her upper arm jiggles and wishes there was a health club in town. She grins—that grin of hers never aged. Her lips will always stay famous when the rest of her falls away. Health club in town? She wishes there was still a town at all.

The morning crowd nods and touches her arm and says "howdy" and "hey-now" as she pushes through them to the door. Saint Frankie of the Perpetual Coffeepot. She unlocks the door with those jangling keys, rattling and melodious. She feels like a fifth-grade schoolteacher and they feel like kids waiting for school to start. The men look her over. She still fills a pair of jeans, they think, though only she knows what size she wears now. The swinging door allows the old scents of grease and bread and donuts and eggs to join the sage and dust in the street. The breakfast club follows Frankie into the shadows, seeking refuge.

Frankie flips on the a.c. and the blowers bang to life.

They think they've always been there, these good people, but they haven't. One of her breakfast club, Ike, used to tell Shoshone tales to anyone who would listen. He was a major pain, of course, with his Indian legends. But then he died and suddenly became one of their angels. *Good ol' Ike! And Remember when Ike used to say . . . ?* And what he said was that the cliffs did not love them because they spoke English, not Shoshone. That the spirits who tended to the butte spoke the old tongue, and nobody who ever climbed up there managed to learn a damn word of Shoshone—he always pronounced it *Sho-shown,* like that. "If you learned a few old songs and went up there to sing, the mountains would hear you, and miracles would happen." He smoked two packs a day like all the old-timers, and he died in 1987.

But the cliffs are older than the Sho-shown. The cliffs don't count years—years are seconds to them. Flecks of gypsum pushed off the edge by the hot wind. They are the original inhabitants of this valley. And they weren't always cliffs. They were entire mountains once, until the inevitable carving wind and scouring dust and convulsive earthquakes and cracking ice trimmed them, thinned them, made their famous face appear to oversee the scurrying of those below.

Mountains, too, are doomed to die. But it is their curse to die more slowly than anything else on earth. To weaken and fall, mile by mile, carrying their arrowheads into the gullies, and with them the gemstone skeletons of the old ones, and the great stony spines of the elder giants. Even these are mere infants to the falling mountains. All falling as grit on the flats. Tiny hills for ants to climb.

*

If you hit Highway 20 to Idaho Falls, you've already missed it: New Junction—home of the Benson Hill High School Mountain Men and the State Champion Benson Hill Colorettes. The sign on the playing field is partly down now. It says:

SON HI

OLO ETT S

Frankie's Diner is the only restaurant left in town, though there is a Taco John's on the east side, right before you hit the Sinclair station with its green dinosaur on the sign. The mountains knew those animals well. Truckers and tourists, when they come through, stop at Taco John's for their sodas and their burritos and their toilet breaks. Frankie doesn't seem to mind, though she keeps her feelings close. She doesn't serve hazelnut French roast anyway, she tells herself. Everything at Frankie's is like it ought to be, like it used to be.

She bakes big blueberry muffins every Tuesday and they're gone by dinnertime, mostly gobbled by The Professor and Miss Sally. Frankie's has its best crowds on Tuesday mornings. Everybody comes in except those crusty old waddies who still try to run a few beeves in the draws. Once in a while, one of them rides his horse right down the street, looking like something out of a crazy cowboy movie. They don't even wave, just grimly straddle their saddles and clop out of sight. Those boys don't care to talk much, and if there's one constant at Frankie's, it's palaver. It was busier when she was a kid, when her mom and dad ran the place, but the oil field roustabouts are gone over to Rock Springs in Wyoming. And the uranium miners are long gone, too. Lots of them tearing up the Indian reservations now, but some of them still burning out their lungs and kidneys digging around the back side of the butte. But that's nearer to Arco.

People don't mention Arco much. Hell, Arco came up with the figures on the cliff faces idea before they did. Arco beat the Mountain Men every year just about. Arco was the first city ("city," ha!) lit by nuclear energy in the world. The buttes and mountains look down upon Arco also, and after the seas of molten fire they observed, the reactor meltdown in 1961 was just a little pool.

क्षे

Inside Frankie's, the coffeepot is on and Ralph, the Sinclair owner, sits on his stool at the counter and opens his paper: drunk drivers and abandoned horses and no call for rain. Well, hell—there was never all that much rain to begin with. They are inhabitants of the rain shadow, where those Cascades to the west scrape all the juice out of the clouds as they head this way.

The phone rings, and Frankie beams and sits in the kitchen and says, "Hi, doll! How you feeling?"

"That's Sammy," The Professor says, as if everybody doesn't know it.

"When's she due?" Miss Sally asks.

"Any day now!" The Professor is feeling like a news anchor, delivering the headlines. "A girl!"

"No shit," mutters Ralph.

He's thinking of a vacation. Maybe Florida. He'd like to fish.

They hear her laugh. "Bye-bye!" she says. "Love you too!" Dishes clatter back there.

"Another beautiful day," The Professor announces.

"Wait. Don't tell me," Ralph replies. "It's sunny."

The diner's windows look west, away from the cliffs. Frankie likes it this way. The old motor court sits across the street. And a couple of white houses and two trailers. Some of them have foil over their windows. Satellite dishes. Frankie thinks about how each of those little places is a story. The drivers hurrying through town think about the huge stories looming over the road. They don't

10

even see the town. Those numbers on the face of the butte.

They're huge. Much bigger than the old red handprints painted on the rocks when gargantuan creatures walked the plain, hairy and regal and slow as clouds. Taller than the lines of antelope scratched into the rocks.

The numbers start at 23. They march forward through time and stop at 00. Nobody in town likes to look at 77. Especially Frankie.

✧

"Here we are," Frankie says, as she says every morning, once the call is over.

She pours the first cups.

"How's Sammy?" Sally asks.

"Just about fit to burst," says Frankie.

"I remember those days," Sally says with a wink.

"How did we do it?" says Frankie, going to Ralph, and to the far booth and then to The Professor.

"What the hell," says The Professor at his customary window seat, where he spends every morning staring out— as if there would be anything new to see.

Everybody glances outside, and by damn, something new does come along. A lone steer, all slat sides and idiot drool, ambling down the street, looking in the windows. He stops and chews his cud and drops a pound of fertilizer outside the diner.

Frankie opens the door and waves the coffeepot and scolds, "Shoo, now! G'on!"

He shakes his big horns once and gets dogged on down the street by a squadron of agitated biting flies.

"You seen that?" asks Miss Sally, but nobody answers.

Frankie says to Ralph, "Pay you a dollar to shovel that patty out of there."

Ralph stares at his paper.

"Feed me first. I'll do it when I'm done. No charge. I'll be keeping your tip, though."

"There goes my Cadillac," Frankie says, winking at Sally, who covers her mouth with a napkin.

"A gentleman," The Professor announces. "Chivalry is not dead."

"Sure ain't," says Ralph, pondering the ball scores. God-damned Seahawks.

⌘

Doesn't every town in America have an old-timer called The Professor? That duffer who knows everything and everybody, as long as they are dead. He can tell you who Monica Benson dated between 1955 and her tragic demise in the flood of '67. Yep, it rained sometimes. And the big cliffs made sure the arroyos north of town exploded with deep red floods that swept cars out to the lava beds and left them upside down and full of sand.

Frankie is mixing her batter. The ovens are on. Miss

Sally grabs the pot and goes ahead and refills her friends' cups for them.

"Gotcha, Frankie!" she announces brightly, like another breaking news report.

"Thanks, hon!" Frankie calls from the back.

Everybody has a personal cup, and they hang on wooden dowels on the wall. Old Bev and Howie still hang there, though they died a couple of years ago. Right beside Indian Ike's cup with feathers and a circle with four colors in it.

"Hope you have a hair net!" Frankie adds. Everybody chuckles.

"Oh, you!" cries Sally, which makes her blush as she sits back down.

The Professor's cup has some kind of chemical diagram on it. He really was a professor, of sorts. Taught Science and Bio 101 at Benson Hill. He coached drama club after school, which is where he met Frankie in 1976. It was hard to get boys in there, since actors were pretty much known as "faggots" by the Mountain Men. Still, Frankie was queen of the color guard that year, and some of the footballers followed her naughty smile into the club. That's how he met Son Harding and poor old Stick. Stick made it as an actor for a month and dropped out of the club when he tried to read Shakespeare. That was some fairy shit right there and Stick wasn't going to put up with it. But Frankie and the Colorettes had won a state ribbon that year, and she was hell-bent on winning a drama award, too. She wasn't about to let all the boys off the hook. So Son was her partner—he didn't mind—and they did solos from *West Side Story*. He couldn't sing to save his life, but Frankie belted it out like Skeeter Davis, by God. And she danced fine, too. Spun those skirts of hers like a carnival ride and made everybody feel like it was the Fourth of July when she took the stage. Frankie made Sonny great. They were all juniors that year.

Frankie puts The Professor's bowl of oatmeal in front of him. Sally eats English muffins with jam. She can't afford more, but everyone makes believe she's a light eater. She actually pays with change that she fishes out of one of those plastic ovals that squeeze to open, as if she's still in grade school. Frankie makes a big show every Tuesday of eating a blueberry muffin with her, calling them extras, even though she can't stand them anymore.

Ralph studies the Big Beaner Platter—eggs, chorizo, beans, and tortillas—as if it were an engine needing a tune-up. He isn't sure if Mex food is right for the valley. But he's up for something new.

Professor: "Ralph, what you eating?"

Ralph: "Illegal alien grub."

The Professor turns to three sheepherders skulking in the corner booth, hunched and dark.

"Sorry," he says.

"Basque," says one of them—and a look that tells him to mind his own business. "Legal." The men go back to their eggs.

Professor: "And what you reading?"

14

Ralph: "Paper."

Professor: "What's it say?"

Ralph: "Same as yesterday. Obama's still a communist."

Miss Sally: "Oh now." She still has an old Hillary sign in her front yard. The only blue campaign sign in the whole region.

✌

Frankie's in and out of the swinging door all day long. She tries to count her steps—Dr. Oz says to get in ten thousand a day. She could probably get there on a fairly busy shift. It reminds her of the old marching days. She can't afford busboys right now, so she buses the tables, cooks, washes dishes, and takes the orders. A strand of hair has escaped her braid, and it is stuck to the sweat at her temple. She brushes it away with the inside of her wrist. Her eyes are still blue. No rings on her fingers.

Professor: "You're sweet as a spring daisy."

Frankie: "Sweet-talk me some more and I might run off with you."

She tops off his cup.

"How's the hunt going?" she asks.

"Copacetic."

He loves big words like that. They only piss Ralph off. The three Basque sheep men in the corner eat loud and mumble in their space-alien lingo. They smell like lambs to Frankie.

The Professor has a contract with a scientific catalogue to supply ants for ant farms. He finds a colony and inserts a straw down the hole and blows until the ants swarm out. When they come up with eggs, he knows he's getting somewhere. Sooner or later they evacuate their queen, and he sucks her up in a pipette and puts her in a little plastic container. He makes a few bucks off each container, and he makes a few more for bottles with workers and eggs in them. He has to label the various colonies well so the ants won't find each other when the jars are uncorked and tear each other apart. They go into a cardboard box with perforated holders and go out of Arco via UPS.

He used to man a roadside stand this side of Taco John's where he sold rock crystals and petrified wood he found in a secret canyon up the side of the butte. He had a little sign on his petrified dino dung box: COPROLITES ARE GOOD SHIT. People were probably offended. He sells his rocks on eBay now.

Ralph: "Hunt, hell. Crawling around with your ass in the air. At your age."

"You're a bold talker for a newcomer," The Professor says.

"Been here since nineteen seventy," Ralph says.

The Professor winks at Frankie.

"Dear boy," he says. "I painted the nineteen sixty-three number up on the butte. Used house paint and brand-new rollers that I stole from the janitor's office at Benson Hill. You can't top that."

Ralph rattles the page. He is sick of history. "Congratu-goddamn-lations," he says.

The tradition started in 1923, after the last Indian died up on the butte. They called him Joe, and some cowboy brought him down on a mule. His little valley was where the Class of 1923 made their ascent to paint their graduation date on the lowest available cliff. It was a scandal—the leader of this wild bunch, Billy Pepper, faced a night in the hoosegow until his pap and Mr. Benson himself came and bailed him out. He was mostly in Dutch for drinking, but the town leaders secretly saw a nice tradition being born. The butte knew, if they didn't, that the top of the 23 was at the height where great sharks and whales once swam, and where the smoke of old Joe's last chimney fire hovered as he burned all his letters from his dead wife and his Bible before he lay himself down on the floor of the cabin to sleep forever. Now there is no trace of his house except for the bulbs that break from the ground every April and start to bloom.

The Professor always loved to lecture about the numbers when he subbed the history classes. They weren't in any particular order—24 was right beside 23, but 25 was far off to the west. It depended on the moxie of the painters, didn't it. How high were they brave enough to climb? How long were their ropes? His line was: "Junction's numbers are what hopes and dreams look like." For these were the best moments of their lives. These were the doorways into imagined futures. Doors they thought

17

were swinging wide, though perhaps only their grand-fathers knew the doors were actually slamming behind them.

So 58 abuts 90; 92 bleeds downhill into a feminine-looking 88; 68 is the funny one, but what do you expect? The 8 is two stacked flowers with white petals and yellow hearts—hippies even out here. Some of the numbers seem to have small beards, but these are cascades of dung from peregrine and buzzard nests.

It was 1949 that was the first time people believed the tradition was going to die out. By then, they had made postcards of the numbers, and Frankie's folks sold them in a wire rack beside the cash register. None of the GIs seemed to want to return home. Those Mountain Men who'd made it back from Guadalcanal and Arles were out there bombing around the USA in jalopies and on motor-cycles. Nobody wanted to come punch cows or dig uranium at Arco or try to grow alfalfa or run sheep up on the highlands. That was when the ranches began to die out. Things slowed down, and the first old-timers pronounced The Death of America and The End of the Way Things Were Supposed to Be. But they were off by a few decades. It was really the 1960s that killed them all. Freeways appeared far from New Junction's city limits, and tourists jumped out of the valley and drove the big roads instead, taking their money with them.

Benson Hill closed in 2000. At least Frankie's daughter graduated before that. "Oh my Lord," Frankie thinks. Every once in a while she remembers that she is going to be a grandmother.

She doesn't like it when The Professor talks about all the stories. It just reminds her that 'Junction is blowing away, bit by bit, and Benson Hill is closed and the Colorettes are gone, and the Sinclair with its grand view of the butte is where Stick used to work and she can still see him smoking and staring up at the numbers and then she sees Son in his silly white bell-bottoms. It's not right, is what she thinks. Is a town dead when the old men die, or when the children leave?

Ralph and Miss Sally are playing with The Professor. The numbers game. Frankie wishes she had one of those iPod things to shut their voices out. Son Harding used to like crazy new music back then—Yes and Alice Cooper. She'd listen to that right now if she could.

She drops big blues in front of each client, steaming hot. Dabs of butter running in yellow rivulets down their sides. "One Butte with Lava," she says as she delivers each muffin.

Ralph says, "Nineteen forty-one."

"Oh well. What a year! We were, of course, at war. Benson Hill boys were patriotic, I tell you. They went in high numbers to the Pacific theater."

Frankie is thinking, Sonny always told her he'd take her all the way to the ocean—any ocean—if she'd leave Stick and run away with him. Crazy boy. Wrote her the only poems she ever got from anybody.

The Professor: "That number was painted by a young cowboy with jug ears. Name of Wally Wachtel, known as Big Double for the two W's in his name, don't you know. And his poor old ears. The only big things about Wally were his ears and his hat." He laughs. "Wally undertook that project after the prom. Climbed up there alone. If you were to climb on up there, you'd see across the white number four is the name of his sweetheart, Pru Speich. Poor dumb bastard misspelled 'Pru' and wrote 'P-R-O-O.' Still there. He was shot in the head by a Japanese sniper in the Philippines. His body never came home."

Ralph: "Well, ain't you a bundle of joy."

The Professor: "Natural selection, my friend."

Ralph tosses some money on the counter.

"Christ," he says. "Now it's evolution."

"What a newfangled idea," The Professor mutters.

The butte knows that Big Double Wally saw eagles fly in a mating dance as he struggled up. That he almost fell. That the entire valley floor, once drained of ocean, became another kind of sea—red and orange and screaming hot as the lava rolled across the flats. Ferns, palms, ancient shaggy pines bursting into flame and vanishing under the languid waves of melted stone. Air so hot the flying creatures trying to migrate burst into flame and plunged into the inferno. And Big Double hanging from his little rope, swinging like a pendulum for a minute of sheer terror, shouting, "Oh gravy!"

Miss Sally: "Frankie, dear—your own dad painted the fifty-nine, don't you know."

"Yep. Know it."

Frankie thinks about some of the maneuvers she led the Colorettes through at the games: drop spins, crazy-eight carves, flutters, toaster turns.

Ralph leaves and doesn't shovel the pile outside her door.

⁂

The sun has moved on to that Pacific shoreline she never saw, and it is all probably turning copper and cool at the end of a long day. Here it is still hot, and quiet, and the glow fires up the top half of the butte. She is sitting in her truck, staring at 77, wishing she still smoked. The renegade steer from the morning is lurking beside one of the trailers across the way, and it eyes her, then bellows. She starts her engine and it trots across the street toward her. "What do you think?" she says out loud. "Do I look like a rancher to you?" The steer lows and eyeballs her. She puts the truck in gear. "Do I look like I'm hauling hay to you in some field?" She lowers her window and says, "Shoo." She waves her hand. He shakes his horns and bellows again.

As Frankie drives away, she watches the steer in her rearview, trotting after her.

"Don't you beat all," she says.

She is tired and her feet hurt. That hip is trying to lock up on her again. She thinks she'll be darned if she lets her hip or this crazy little bull keep her from going in-

21

side and watching her shows. She smells like food—it's the worst part of her day. If she washes the grease smell out of her hair, she'll be blow-drying it for hours. Coming home smelling like fried flesh, she can hardly bear to eat. She usually gives herself a bowl of Special K and some iced tea. Watches shows on the satellite where people buy houses on beaches on islands and basically sunburn for a living. She doesn't drink much, but she does have a weakness for a bowl of ice cream. And she likes a hot soak and a good book. But tonight she feels the hollow spot, and she drops a splash of Southern Comfort into her Diet Coke and then another.

Outside, the chain-link rattles. Stupid cow.

"You better not eat my flowers," she says.

She laughs for a minute—what is the neighbor going to think when she sees Frankie has a new bull?

It's time for her bath. She has a good mystery she's been working on—a Sara Paretsky. In those books, Chicago seems like some kind of *Star Wars* city to her, like Oz, if Oz had lots of murders. She can't imagine what it would be like to walk the streets of that giant canyon of crystal and stone. And that lake! Why, they were never going to run out of water. And her daughter. In the city. Just about to pop. Frankie saves calling her for later. "Oh, Sammy," she says. Sammy is the only thing that makes her cry. Sammy and the little peanut she's bringing into the world.

Tub's running. She should save this water for the tree and the steer. When she looks at herself in the mirror, she feels like the drouth has taken all her own water from her, just like the little ranches all about. It takes eight thousand gallons a day to grow enough forage for cattle, and to keep the cows and horses alive.

Her braid looks like straw. Her chin has dropped. Her shoulders are slumping. She cringes when she remembers when Sonny and Stick thought she was the prettiest, most interesting girl in this entire state. How poor Son tried to get her away from Stick. "Your skin is like new snow," he'd tell her. What kind of thing was that to say? It must have come out of his books he was always carrying around. Nobody talked like that. Not to Frankie. It shook her, bad.

The picture of Son is in the hallway, outside the bathroom. She touches his face when she goes to bed. He had the softest hair she ever felt, on a girl or a boy. She always wishes she could touch that hair one more time. Poor old Stick hangs in the kitchen, beside the fridge.

She calls Sammy most nights, but the Southern Comfort has made her sleepy. Besides, sometimes Frankie senses that she bores her daughter. And Frankie can't bear to be boring anymore. Frankie says a prayer every night and settles in to listen to the all-night UFO shows on the AM radio.

On her left hip, where nobody sees it, her only tattoo: *1977*.

Stickshift, so they called him—on account of his ability to drive anything with a motor—never forgave Sonny for leaving the Mountain Men. He probably suspected Frankie and Sonny had some secret thing going on in the little theater, but then Son was just a drama fag. Right? Shit, they probably shared lipstick and pantyhose! Haw. The boys laughed at that.

Frankie was loyal to Stick, of course. They were going to marry after school ended. Stick was going to run the gas station and expand the garage beside it to service all the cars and tractors and trucks between here and Boise. He wasn't much of a reader, unlike Frankie, but he brought her paperbacks when he went on runs with his dad, delivering machine parts into Oregon. Sonny, though. Sonny came at her with poems and paintings and drawings and records. Son smelled her hair and teased her till she laughed so hard she cried. And they acted together like they were dancing.

But even Frankie's dad said Son was no-account. A hippie. "You can't eat poems," he told her.

It was after the senior prom when Son came up to her at the bonfire at the foot of the cliffs. Everybody was drinking. Stick was blitzed and sleeping in his truck. The Colorettes were roasting marshmallows for the boys. And Sonny sidled up to her and smelled her neck. The bolts of lightning that shot down her body made her jump. Somebody was playing Seger on the tape deck. They locked eyes.

"Frankie," he said. "Run away with me."

She shoved him a little.

24

"Crazy boy."

"No, seriously. Let's run away. Portland. I want to take you to that beach."

She laughed.

"You're drunk."

He kissed her lips.

She stared into his eyes.

"What are you doing?" she whispered.

"I don't know."

He sipped his beer.

"Can I do it again?"

"No!"

They kissed, hard. She bit his lips.

Son's breath was shaking out of him, and they leaned against each other—the huge perpetual shadow of the cliff looming over the entire town, the bottoms of the numbers writhing in the fire's light as if they were dancing.

"I want to touch your hair," she said.

Stick staggered out of the dark and he and Son stood side by side, peeing on the cliff face.

The Colorettes shrieked, "Ooh! Gross!" and scurried about in a frenzy of faux panic.

Stick hugged Son.

"You ain't so bad," he said. Went back to sleep some more.

Later, Frankie's hands clutched Son's hair and she cried against his bare shoulder. And ever since, she has thought she should have run. She should have gone. But you can't just quit. You can't just leave home behind to wither and die. You can't. You can't.

She drinks.

⊘

The empty house sits in the silent morning. The yearbook is still on the table, but the coffee cup is in the drainer. Outside, the little bull rakes his horns across the chain-link fence and, after a while, gives up and walks away. Nobody sees him go.

Above Frankie's house, a slab of numbers wants to fall. Ice has gradually pried it loose from the butte, and it is just a matter of time until it shatters in a storm of rock. Could be today, could be in a hundred years.

Inside the diner, Frankie's telephone is ringing.

The breakfast club has begun to gather. It's just The Professor and Ralph and Sally. No sheepherders.

The Professor: "Know what a dinosaur is?"

Ralph: "No, what?"

Professor: "It's a sore you get from sitting around in a diner all day! Get it?"

Sally: "Did you just make that up?"

Ralph: "Know what a seven-course cowboy breakfast is?"

Professor: "No, what?"

Ralph: "A six-pack and a fistfight."

Sally: "I wonder where that girl's at."

They check their watches.

∽

Frankie had wanted to go to Bible school for a couple of years and come back to marry Stick and teach Sunday school at Christ the Redeemer. Stick wasn't into no college—he had his business all lined up, and his folks fronted him the money for a nice little house right outside town, where antelopes moved by like small sailboats in the golden grasses, and a family of foxes had a den in a little cut bank not a quarter mile from the back porch. But Son was going on to State, and he was going to read poems for gosh sakes. Poems. What was he going to do with poems? He drove her crazy sometimes.

"I'm going to *live*," he proclaimed. As if she wasn't alive. As if he'd be so much more alive than anybody else. It made her mad.

That night, he and Stick stole the paints from the Benson Hill janitor's room. Two cans of house paint.

They climbed together in the dark. It rained. Everybody remembers that rain, how different it was that rain came in so late in the spring. And they must have made it because the big yellow 77 was there, far above the other numbers. Those boys crawling up the rock in the storm, probably egging each other on. Probably competing. The numbers are so high, no one has ever climbed up there to look, but everyone's certain one of the sevens says *Frankie*. And people speculate still on which hand painted it.

Frankie is grateful she wasn't the one who found them, lying broken at the foot of the butte. It was Stick's poor father. He covered them with his coat and a tarp from the truck before he staggered out of there, forgetting to drive, hollering for somebody to get the sheriff.

⬦

Little pebbles drop from the Shoshone butte and sound like rain hitting Frankie's tin roof. At the diner, they press their faces to the glass and peer into the dark, as if she might have somehow snuck past and entered without their noticing. They hear the phone ringing and ringing until it stops.

"I'm starving," The Professor says.

Miss Sally says, "What if…"

Dirt rolls down the street. It makes small patterns in the wind that almost look like little waves.

Once, when the valley was full of water, dragonflies as big as ravens rattled through ferns and tall spikes of grasses and cattails. Cool fog blanketed the face of the butte—the softest thing the valley had ever known. Sometimes, the last people of New Junction dream of it: fog. It comes to them like a memory they never had. It is the dream of the mountains. The word for fog that none of them know sounds like the pinging of pebbles on Frankie's roof. If only someone could say it, miracles might happen. The numbers hover in the haze. Peregrines dive. And the Shoshone word for the lost cool fog is *pogonip*.

The Professor looks up. "She'll be here," he says. "Right? Right?"

Ralph is already walking away.

Two

The Southside Raza Image Federation Corps of Discovery

So this was New Year's Day. This was sunlight. Seventy-eight degrees. This was the sound of the barrio awakening from the party: doves mourning the passing of night, pigeons in the dead palm trees chuckling amid rattling fronds, the mockingbird doing car alarm and church bell iterations in Big Ángel's olive trees in front of the house. Junior pulled the pillow over his head—it was those kids with their Big Wheels making all that noise.

Somebody knocked on the screen door.

Junior groaned, rolled out of bed. He was in his plaid boxers. Yeah, he was skinny, but he was working out after school every day. Big Ángel wasn't worth much lately, but he did put cement in two coffee cans and sink a bar in the middle so Junior could curl and get his guns pumped. He flexed in the mirror. Guns! More like derringers.

Bam-bam-bam on the screen door.

"A'ight, güey! I'm coming!"

The living room was covered in sleeping vatos. They

were tangled on the couch and on the floor and there were dead forties and vino bottles scattered all over. The TV was still on: ESPN2. Junior shook his head. His big brother, Little Ángel, was snoring. That damned Chango was on the floor. Junior gave him a little kick and shot Chango the bird as he stepped over him.

"I seen that," Chango warned, though his eyes never opened.

They'd started arriving last night around ten. Poor old Big Ángel's first New Year's without Moms in the house. He'd invited them to enjoy the fridge and the eggnog and had gone off to bed.

"Egg knobs?" Chango had said. "What the fuck's an egg knob?"

This is why Junior did everyone's homework for them— he was only in tenth grade, but the seniors were doomed without his help. "Dude likes to read!" was the insult they threw at him, and of course he was forced to deny it. He hid his paperbacks under his bed. Still, they relied on Junior's smarts to pass their classes, so they didn't beat him up so much. Sometimes, though, Chango and Little Ángel shoved him in a kitchen cabinet and put a broomstick through the handles, leaving him till the old man woke up and let him out.

Junior squinted out onto the porch.

There he stood. Hair all crazy like some kind of hippie. Shadow García.

"There he is," said Junior.

Shadow shouted Junior's name, using that fake Beaner accent he enjoyed when he was mocking everybody: "WHO-nyurr!" he bellowed.

Junior scratched his butt.

"Qué?" he said.

"Let's go to the beach, ese."

Junior squinted.

"For reals?"

"Why not? You the only one awake, peewee."

Junior grinned.

"Let me get my flip-flops," he said.

Shadow lit a smoke and bounced on the balls of his feet.

"Uh-huh, homey. Bring a li'l bucket too, an' like a blow-up dragon an' shit," he said. "Shit!" He cracked himself up.

ϑ̵ϕ

The shirts were out of style, but the homeboys still had respect. It was poor old Big Ángel's thing, that veterano thing, where the old guys thought a lowrider car was the point, a zoot suit maybe, and a fine placa for the back window with a cool logo. They had gothic T-shirts printed, sleeveless, and Junior wore his. *Southside Raza Image Federation Y QUE c/s* in a double rocker-arch around a drawing of a loco wolf with a bandana around his brow and a gold tooth winking in his mouth. The lobo was saying "Orale!" and holding up a doobie.

"Lots of Chicano historical data in that shirt," said

Shadow as he steered his mom's station wagon. The radio was where it should be: zeroed in on the oldies station. They didn't go for that Lady Ca Ca stuff or that pinche gangsta crap.

Junior was slumped back in his seat, riding shotgun. He was burningly aware of the two girlies in the backseat, La Smiley and La Li'l Mousey. They were popping their gum, bored as always, filling the car with perfume. Hair all ratted out.

"Las morras back there got raccoon eyes," Shadow confided.

Junior glanced back at the girls. The Sotomayor sisters. Damn. Their eyes were outlined in black.

"What?" said Mousey. "Mind your business, boy."

He turned back and grinned at Shadow.

"You like that?" Shadow asked.

"Well, yeah."

"You in love, vato!"

"I'm in love with the world!"

Shadow hooted out the window. "My man!" he said, nodding and jittering in the driver's seat. "My ma-a-an."

He honked the horn.

†p

They drove out to the Silver Strand. It seemed like all San Diego and all Chula Vista and half of National City were heading for the beach. Fat moms and swabbies from the naval air base and old farts in big Hawaiian shirts and all those wetbacks from Tijuana. The vatos didn't like the fuckin' wetbacks, that was for sure. Sureños from the south battled it out with Norteños from the north; Chicanos faced off against Mexicanos. Beaners versus rednecks. Everybody against the black brothers. And just forget about the Asians. It was natural selection, just as they had learned from Darwin as explained by Professor Junior. Nobody liked nobody.

"Yo, Junior," Shadow said as he parked in the sandy lot across the highway from the beach. "What we reading next in Mr. Hitler's class?"

Mr. Hitler. Junior snickered. That friggin' Shadow.

"We're reading about Lewis and Clark."

"What's up with Lewis and Clark?"

"They, like, took canoes and rowed all across America and checked shit out for the president."

"No shit? Like who, Reagan?"

"No, ese. A real old dude. It was a hundred years ago."

"Reagan, like I said!" Shadow announced.

He jumped out of the car, circling to the back door.

"Ladies," he said, holding their door open. He was swooping on La Smiley—everybody knew it. Junior was worried: La Li'l Mousey was too much woman for him, he was sure of it.

"Did Louie and Clark find dinosaurs?" Shadow asked.

"You crazy."

"Read that book, boy!" (Who, Shadow?)

La Mousey terrified Junior by putting her arm around his waist.

They walked to the tunnels under the roadway. Jet fighters patrolled the beach on their way to North Island. Border Patrol helicopters appeared and disappeared to the south. The concrete tunnels were sandy. People had tagged inside them—blurry messages and pictures nobody paid attention to.

Two shadowy thugs were coming their way, and Junior didn't even look at them, he was so enraptured by Shadow and so sweaty under La Mousey's arm. The first thug slammed his shoulder into Shadow as he passed. Shadow bounced off the tunnel wall. The thug said, "Lárgate, pocho."

"What did you say to me, bitch?" said Shadow.

"Pocho puto," the thug replied.

Mexicans.

Shadow smiled. "You come into my country and talk smack to me? Really? Really? Okay." He nodded. "Sure, why not."

Shadow fired a right fist straight into the thug's ribs and followed with a left that knocked him off his feet— shoes sliding out from under him on the sand-covered cement. His head clonked like a coconut when he went down.

"Shadow! Shadow!" Junior yelled. The girlies backed to the wall and shrieked with pleasure.

"Do him, Junior! Do him good!" Shadow yelled as he

kicked and punched the other Mexican to the ground. Junior turned to the fallen thug, who was groggy but rising. He drew back his foot, pausing for a second to consider his black Converse, then kicked the thug in the mouth.

♒

"I'ma barf," Junior said as they spun out of the lot and hurried toward the freeway. Shadow was crazy-happy, bloody knuckles and all. He punched the ceiling.

"You ain't gonna barf!"

"I'ma barf," Junior said.

"You whipped that asshole but good, peewee!" Shadow hollered. "He's in love with the world!" he shouted. "Hey—don't barf. You do not barf in my mom's car."

Li'l Mousey leaned over the seat and massaged Junior's shoulders.

"Junior?" she said. "You okay?"

He groaned.

"Honey," she said, "you got a tooth stuck in your shoe."

He barfed.

Shadow shrieked, "Not in my mom's car, homes! Damn!"

"Sorry," mumbled the professor as they sped back to the 'hood.

♒

The next morning Junior was in bed reading *The Stand* when that knock came again on the screen door. For a moment, he considered not answering. But he did.

Shadow. Bloodshot eyes.

"Heavyweight Champion of the World!" Shadow said.

Chango had wanted to hang the Mexican's tooth on a thong so Junior could wear it like some Apache warrior.

"Sup?" said Junior.

"Sup with you?"

Junior shrugged.

"Aquí nomás," he said. "Sup with you?"

"Nuttin. I don't know. Sup?"

"Hangin'."

"I hear that." They stared at each other through the screen.

"Chillin'," Shadow offered. "After the big fight."

Junior chuckled.

"Tha's right," he said. He made a muscle.

"No shame in your game!" Shadow announced.

They smiled.

"Um, I got you somethin'," Shadow said.

"Yeah?"

"Like a prize or some shit, right?" Shadow reached into his back pocket and pulled out a flimsy little pink paperback. "Check that out. I di'nt get a word of it, but I know you like that crazy stuff."

Junior opened the screen and took the book. It was a

bent and battered *Trout Fishing in America*. He already had one under his bed.

"Brautigan," he said.

"Is that how you say it?" Shadow asked.

"Thanks."

Shadow bounced a little in place.

"I got you something better, homes."

"Yeah?"

"Simón, güey. Step out here."

Junior stepped out on the porch.

"Check it," Shadow said, pointing to his mom's station wagon. It had an aluminum canoe tied to the roof. "Sweet, right?"

"Shadow!" said Junior. "Where'd you get that?"

"I stole it!"

"What?"

"I went out driving. I can't sleep, man. Can you? I can't. Yo, so I went driving, right? They got this Boy Scout camp up on Otay Mesa. Around the lake. Like, all these tents with sleeping Scouts. I snuck in and stole it. For you!"

"You're crazy!"

"I stole some paddles, too. They're in the car."

They regarded the canoe.

"What are we supposed to do with a canoe?" Junior asked.

Shadow smiled.

"Louie and Clark, homes. Like, let's go discovering."

❧

The marshes and creeks were to the east and the south of Big Ángel's house. Between the barrio and the border, pretty much. The sloughs.

Back in the day, crabs were attracted to the clotted blood-water that oozed out of the little slaughterhouse about a quarter mile from the gravel parking lot at the bottom of the barrio hill. Big Ángel could catch some supper down in there. Nowadays, nobody went down there except maybe Chango. If Chango was there, nobody else wanted to go there. But Shadow could take Chango any day or night.

They carted the canoe over their heads, the gunnels breaking their shoulders. It weighed about nine hundred pounds, in Junior's opinion. "How can a piece of shit that weighs as much as a car," Shadow wanted to know, "float on the water?" They staggered down the dirt road and skirted the gravel lot. Old motor oil in the dust still gave up its aroma of engines. Soda cans crushed flat in the gravel had faded pale orange in the relentless sunlight. Somebody had spray-painted tags on an old truck. Grasshoppers burst out of the weeds as the boys advanced, blasting through the air with clackety ratchet sounds. Jimmy noted the rolling passage of a tumbleweed.

Across the sloughs, the little slaughterhouse almost looked nostalgic. Occasional tides of blood and offal still pulsed out of there, making the sloughs stink worse than usual. It looked like the blood wasn't flowing that morning.

They heaved the canoe into the sludge that passed for water, and it hit with a flat smack. Shadow had to push it with his foot, hopping along until it seemed like it was bobbing. They watched to see if it would sink.

"There you go!" Shadow said. "Hop in!"

He steadied it, and Junior climbed in. Then Shadow climbed in. Their weight sank the bottom of the canoe into the muck and they sat there, moored like a commemorative statue of two idiots setting out for an adventure.

"Okay," said Shadow. "So we ain't Lewis and Clark."

They got out. The rancid blood-mud released the canoe with great sucking reluctance. They portaged it around the hill to the busted end of Half-Hill Road. The water there was almost four feet deep. They put in again and found themselves floating.

"Holy shit!" cried Shadow.

It took them a few minutes to coordinate their oarsmanship, but they finally made forward motion after a little floundering. Junior was in front and Shadow squatted in back. They moved down one of the braided waterways, scraping between crumbling humps of weeds and mud. A green crab threatened Shadow from one black bank. Junior looked down into the water. He could see rainbows of pollution and oil on the surface, and weird billows of yellow and green filth that rose from the gray bottom like small poisoned geysers.

They maneuvered around a slime-covered shopping cart. Junior pointed out a washing machine in the water. Corduroy pants on a hillock, brittle after years in the sun. They squeezed through a narrow passage and were startled to find themselves in a bigger stream. A heron raised its head and regarded them with disdain.

"Big fuckin' bird!" Shadow shouted.

The heron raised its wings and left the earth in slow motion and hove upstream.

"What's that?" Junior said, leaning over.

"That's like," Shadow said, "that's like freakin' shrimps down there!"

They watched evil-looking white crustaceans scuttle out from under the shadow of their boat.

"Dude," said Junior. "That's totally awesome."

"No disrespect or nothin'," Shadow replied, "but you're talkin' like a white boy. You a vato or a gabacho?"

They paddled down to the railroad bridge, ducked their heads, and made their way under it, horrified by the vast networks of spiderwebs under there. A baseball cap floated in an eddy. "Because," Shadow said, "you got to be something. If you ain't something, you're nothing. That's a fact."

They kept cutting south as they paddled west. They went into the darkness under I-5, where they could hear the whoosh of the cars overhead, the thrum when trucks went by. The whole bridge clanged and clicked. When they busted out of the shadows, close to the southern bank, they could see broken old buildings. White birds standing in the water. Bright yellow flowers formed a fluorescent haze on the bank.

"That's mustard," Shadow said.

"No way."

"Yes sir! Mustards come from, like, flowers. You didn't know that?"

Shadow Boone, Barrio Naturalist.

Junior looked down.

"Fish!" he cried.

"Oh shit!"

Under the boat there was a little swirl of curious sunfish.

"Check it out," Shadow said. He dangled a finger in the water and wiggled it. Several of the fish rushed over and tried to nibble it. This delighted Shadow, and he insisted on playing this game with the fish, even though his antics threatened to capsize the canoe. Junior waited him out, and after a while they resumed paddling. "I'ma come back as a fish when I die," Shadow said. "I'ma be a big fat catfish. How about you, peewee?"

"I'm not coming back," said Junior.

Shadow paddled.

"That's deep," he finally said.

They were going far now. They couldn't even see the hill anymore. Total silence. Junior looked up on the bank. Bushes and planks and boxes and a lean-to.

"Shadow," he said. "Check it out."

As they floated by, carried now by the current, they saw faces staring out at them from the bushes. Gaunt, haunted faces. Silent Mexican men hiding from the Border Patrol. Waiting for night. One raised his hand in a silent greeting.

Shadow and Junior dug in with their paddles and moved downstream.

They paddled past a wrecked car sitting beneath a bare tree. Chickens scratched around the chassis. Suddenly, they broke out into an even bigger body of water. To the south, they saw the skeletal towers of the power station.

"The sea!" shouted Shadow.

"That's not the sea," said Junior. "This is the cooling pond. Big Ángel used to go fishing here."

They let the canoe drift while they ate their sandwiches.

A sea turtle broke the surface of the water and blew air at them.

"Jesus Christ!" shouted Shadow.

Junior had heard about this—the turtles congregated around the power station, enjoying the warm water. He was about to tell Shadow all about it when a Border Patrol helicopter roared overhead, made a sharp turn, and swooped down upon them.

☙

White trucks skidded to a stop on the banks and bullhorns commanded them to beach the canoe. Shadow was mouthing off before he even got out of the boat. "Fuckin' racists! I'm an American citizen! That's right! That's right! You can't do shit to me, gringos cabrones! I am USA all the way!" he raised his fists. "USA, all the way! USA, all the way!"

But it turned out he wasn't USA all the way at all. When the Border Patrol agents got them to the station, they discovered that Shadow García was illegal. He'd been born in Tijuana and his parents had snuck him over the border as an infant. He'd been in the USA illegally all this time and never knew it.

"But I ain't no Mexican," he said. "I'm a Chicano. I'm a Dodgers fan."

He and his family vanished that night. Junior never saw Shadow again. He sat through "Mr. Hitler's" endless droning lectures, taking notes for those failures, Chango and Little Ángel. But he never did read Louie and Clark. And he never again went downhill to the gravel lot.

Shadow wasn't the kind of guy who sent postcards. And sooner or later everyone forgot all about him. And Junior never mentioned him again. He never did find out what happened to that pinche canoe.

Three

The National City
Reparation Society

It wasn't like Junior only hung with white people now. But he didn't see much Raza, he'd be the first to admit. Not socially. That's why you leave home, right? Shake off the dark.

As soon as he picked up the clamoring cell phone, he had that old traditional homecoming feeling: Why'd I answer this? He didn't recognize the number—some old So Cal digits. He stared at the screen for a moment, as if it would offer him further clues.

An accented voice said:

"Hey, bitch."

"Excuse me?"

"Said: Hey. Bitch. You deaf, homes?"

"You must have the wrong number," Junior said, about to click off. *Homes,* he said to himself. *What is this, nineteen eighty-six?*

"Junior!" the guy shouted. He used the old hectoring fake-Beaner accent the vatos had affected when mocking him in school: WHO-nyurr! "I bet you got some emo shit for a ringtone. Right? Like 'The Black Parade,' some shit like that." The guy laughed.

"I've been talking to you for, like, one and a half minutes, and you already insulted me. I don't even know who you are." He knew who it was—he just didn't want to talk to him.

His ringtone was Nine Inch Nails, thank you very much. Emo! Shit.

"I'm out, 'homes.'"

He clicked off and pulled on his Pumas. Got his jog on along the beach. It was one of those rare sunny days, and everybody was out looking in their Lycra and spandex like a vast roving fruit salad. He tucked the celly in his shorts pocket. Who's the bitch now, he wanted to know.

His nemesis caught him again as he was cooling off, jogging in place beside a picnic table, breathing through his nose, pouring good clean sweat down his back—he could feel it trickling down the backs of his legs. "You let me penetrate you," his phone announced. "You let me desecrate you."

"You again?" Junior said.

"It's me! Damn! It's Chango!"

Junior wiped his face with the little white towel he had wrapped around his neck.

"Yeah. Right? I should have known an' all."

"That's what I'm sayin'."

"Fucking Chango."

"Right?"

Junior could hear Chango smoking—he still must like those cheap-ass Domino ciggies from TJ. They crackled like burning brush when Chango inhaled.

"Why you calling me, Chango?"

"What—a homeboy can't check on his li'l peewee once in a while? I like to make sure my boyz is okay."

"I haven't talked to you in ten years," Junior said. He sat on the tabletop and lay back and watched the undersides of gulls as they hung up there like kites.

"So?" said Chango. "You think you're better than us now, college boy?"

Apparently the one thousand–mile buffer zone was not enough barrier between himself and the old homestead.

"Nice talking to you, Chango. Be sure to have someone send me an invitation to your funeral. So long. Have a nice day."

"Hey, asshole," Chango said. "I'm gonna live forever. Gonna be rich, too. I'm workin' on a plan—cannot fail. You gon' want some of this here."

"A plan?" Junior said.

And when he said it, he felt the trap snap shut over him and he couldn't quite figure out how or why he was caught.

⊕

It was a short flight. Lindbergh was clotted with GIs in desert camo and weepy gals waving little plastic American flags. Junior caught the rental-car bus and grabbed a Kia at Alamo. No, he wasn't planning to take it across the border. Put it on the Visa, thanks. Oh, well—the homies were going to give him shit about the car. It would be badass if they rented '67 Impalas with hydraulic lifters so he could enter the barrio with his right front tire raised in the air like some kind of saluting robot. He didn't smile—he was already thinking like Chango! He poked at the radio till he found 91X and The Mighty Oz was cranking some Depeche Mode. At least there was that.

On his way south, he hopped off the freeway, onto Sports Arena, but Tower Records was gone. What? He pulled a U and tried again, as if he'd somehow missed the store. Gone? How could it be gone? Screw that—he sped to Washington and went up to Hillcrest and looked for Off the Record. He was in the mood for some import CDs. Keep his veneer of sanity. It was gone, too. Junior sat there in the parking lot where the Hillcrest Bowl used to be. He could not believe it—all culture had vanished from San Diego. His phone said, "You let me penetrate you." Chango. Junior didn't answer.

He'd only come to check it out. It was a crazy adventure, he told himself. Good for a laugh. Chango had picked up a magazine in a dentist's office. New dentures: our tax dollars at work. He thought it was a *Nat Geo*, but he wasn't sure. Some gabacho had written an article about abandoned homes along the I-15 corridor. Repos. Something like six out of ten, maybe seven out of fifteen or something like that. Point was, they were just sitting there, like haunted houses, like the whole highway was a long ghost town, and the writer had broken in to look around and found all kinds of stuff just laying around. Sure, sad shit like kids' homework on the kitchen table. But it's on a kitchen table, you catch my drift, Chango demanded. There's whole houses full of furniture and mink coats and plasma TVs and freakin' Bose stereos. La-Z-Boys! Hells yeah! Some have cars in the garages. And it's all foreclosed and owned by some bank. But the kicker—the kicker, Yuniorr—is that the banks can't afford to resell this stuff, so they send trucks to the houses to haul the stuff to the dump. Friggin' illegals driving trucks just drag it all out and go toss it. A million bucks' worth of primo swag. "You tell me, how many freakin' apartments gots big-screen TVs that them boys just hauled home? You been to the swap meet?" And Chango had noted, in his profound research (he stole the magazine from the dentist's), that the meltdown had banks backed up. Some of these houses wouldn't be purged for a year or more.

"Ain't even stealin', peewee. Nobody wants it anyway. Worst case is breaking and entering. So I got this plan and I'm gonna make us a million dollars in a couple of months. But I need you to help."

"Why me?"

"You know how to talk white. Shit! Why'd you think?"

Junior motored down I-5 and dropped out at National City. He was loving the tired face of America's finest city—San Diego was a'ight, but National was still the bomb. The Bay Theater, where he used to see Elvis revivals and Mexican triple features. He'd kissed a few locas up there in the back rows. He smiled. He checked the old Mile of Cars—they used to call it The Mile of Scars, because sometimes Shelltown or Del Sol dudes would catch them out there at night and fists would fly between the car lots. That was before everybody got all gatted up and brought the 9s along. Junior shook his head; he would have never imagined that fistfights and fear would come to seem nostalgic.

He drove into the old 'hood, heading for W. 20th and Chango's odd crib over the hump and hiding behind the barrio on the little slope to the old slaughterhouse estuaries. He wanted to see his old church, maybe light a candle. He never meant to go all "mi vida loca" in his life. He didn't mean to go so far away and not come back, either. St. Anthony's. America's prettiest little Catholic church. He smiled. They'd sneak out of catechism and go down behind the elementary school and play baseball on the edge of the swamp. There was a flat old cat carcass they used for home plate.

He turned the corner and beheld an empty lot surrounded by a low chain-link fence. He slammed on the brakes. It was gone, like Tower Records. Things seemed to be vanishing as if all of San Diego County were being abducted by aliens.

He jumped out of his car and watched a man watering his lawn, surrounded by a platoon of pug dogs.

"Where's the church?" he called.

"Burned down! Where you been?"

"What? When?"

"Long time, long time. Say, ain't you that García boy?"

"Not me," said Junior, getting back in the car.

He drove past his old house. Man, it sure looked tiny. Looked like all his old man's gardens were dead. He didn't want to look at it. It had a faded FOR SALE sign stuck in the black iron fence.

The barrio had a Burger King in it, and a Tijuana Trolley stop. Damn. All kinds of Mexican nationals sat around on the cement benches savoring their Quata Poundas among squiggles of graffiti. Junior shook his head.

He dropped into the ancient little underpass and popped out on the west side of I-5 and hung a left and went to the end of the earth and hung another left and dropped down the small slope toward the black water and there it was. Chango's house. His dad's old, forgotten Esso station. Out of business since 1964. Chango lived in the triangular office. He'd pasted butcher paper over the glass and had put an Obama poster on the front, with some Sharpie redesigns so that it now said:

CHANGO YOU CAN BELIEVE IN

He'd given the pres a droopy pachuco mustache and some tiny, irritating homeboy sunglasses. Junior knew that Chango, ever the classicist, would still call the glasses

57

"gafas." He knocked on the glass until Chango woke up from his nap.

✍

"Car's for shit," Chango noted as Junior drove.

"Where we going?" Junior said.

"You remember the Elbow Room? That's where we're goin'. Down behind there. Hey, the radio sucks, ese. What's this? You should be listening to oldies."

Junior punched the OFF button.

"Damn," Chango muttered. "Shit." He looked like a greasy old crow. All wizened and craggy, all gray and lonesome. His big new teeth were white and looked like they were made out of slivers of oven-safe bakeware. His fingers were yellow from decades of Mexican cigarettes. "For reals," he was saying. It was apparently a long-standing conversation he had with himself. His various jail tattoos were purple and blurry and could have been dice rolling snake eyes and maybe a skeleton with a sombrero and on the other forearm an out-of-focus obscenity. He had that trustworthy little vato loco cross tattooed in the meat between his thumb and forefinger. "Tha's right, you know it," he said.

He'd shown Junior the article. It was by Charles Bowden, and did, indeed, confess to uninvited recon sorties into the creepy abandoned homes. One found these places by looking for overgrown yellow lawns and a sepulchral silence.

They pulled around the old block where everybody used to drink at the Elbow Room, except for Junior, who was too young to get in. They rattled around into a dirt alley and Chango directed him to stop at the double doors of a garage. They could hear Thee Midniters blasting out.

"That's some real music, boy," Chango said, and creaked out of his seat, though he managed to sway pretty good once he got erect, swaggering like an arthritic pimp.

Inside, a Mongol associate of Chango's had dolled up a stolen U-Haul panel truck. He wore his vest and scared Junior to death, though lots of vatos liked the Mongols because they were the only Chicano bikers around.

"Sup?" the Mongol said.

"Sup?" Junior nodded.

"Sup?" said Chango.

"Hangin'," said the Mongol.

There was a time when Junior would have written a poem about this interaction and turned it in for an easy A in his writing workshop. *Oh, Junior, you're so street, as it were.*

The van was sweet, he had to admit. It was painted white. It had a passable American eagle on each side, clutching a sheaf of arrows and a bundle of dollars in its claws. Above it: BOWDEN FEDERAL and some meaningless numbers in smaller script. Below it: *Reclamation and Reparation/Morgage Default Division.*

Junior was all caught up in dreams of a little house and a lot of books. Junior wasn't all that interesting. He wanted a garden. He was tired of the game. All he needed was some real money.

He stared at the truck.

"You misspelled 'mortgage,'" Junior said, shaking his head.

They gawked.

"So what?" Chango said. "Cops can't spell."

"The plates are from Detroit," the Mongol pointed out. "An associate UPS'd 'em to me yesterday." He turned to Chango. "Your sedan is out back."

Chango bumped fists with him.

"Remember, I want a fifty-inch flat screen."

"Gotcha."

"And any fancy jewelry and coats for my old lady."

"Gotcha, gotcha."

"And any stash you find."

"You get the chiba, I got it. But I'm drinkin' all the tequila I find."

Chango, in his element.

chp

Junior had to admit, it was so stupid it was brilliant. It was just like acting. He had learned this in his drama workshop. You sold it by having complete belief. You inhabited the role and the viewers were destined to believe it, because who would be crazy enough to make up such elaborate lies?

He followed the truck up I-15 in a sweet Buick with

stolen Orange County plates. Black, of course. He wore a Sears suit and a striped tie. His name tag read MR. PETRUCCI.

"Here's the play. We move shit—we're Beaners," Chango explained. "Ain't nobody gonna even look at us. You're the boss. You're Italian. As long as you got a suit and talk white, ain't nobody lookin' at you, neither."

To compound the play—to sell the illusion, his college self whispered—he had a clipboard with bogus paperwork clipped to it, state tax forms they had picked up at the post office.

Three guys in white jumpsuits bobbed along in the cab of the truck—Chango, a homeboy named Hugo, and the driver, Juan Llaves. Hugo was a furniture deliveryman, so he knew how to get heavy things into a truck. They banged north, dropping out of San Diego's brown cloud of exhaust and into some nasty desert burnscape. They took an exit more or less at random and pulled down several mid-Tuesday-morning suburban streets—all sparsely planted with a palm here, an oleander there. Plastic jungle gyms in yellow yards, hysterical dogs appalled by the truck, abandoned bikes beside flat cement front porches. Juan Llaves pulled into the driveway of a fat faux Georgian half-obscured by weeds and dry grass and looking as dead as a buffalo skull.

Junior took his clipboard in hand and joined Chango on the lawn.

"This is it, Mr. Petrucci!" Chango emoted. Junior

checked his papers and nodded wisely. Nobody even looked out of the neighboring houses. It was silent. "I can't believe we're doing this shit," Chango muttered with a vast porcelain grin.

They tried the front door. Locked. Chango strolled around back. Some clanging and banging and, in a minute, the front door clicked and swung open.

"Electric's off. Hot as hell in here. Fridge stinks."

The associates went inside.

øyp

The bank notices were on the kitchen table. Somebody had abandoned a pile of DVDs on the carpet. "Oh yeah!" Chango hooted. *The Godfather!* Llaves and Hugo hauled the table and chairs out to the truck. Plasma TV in the living room; flat screen in the bedroom. Black panties on the floor looking overwhelmingly sad to Junior. Chango put them in his pocket. "Chango's in love," he told Junior.

In the closet, most of the clothes were gone, but a single marine uniform hung at the back. They took the TVs, a rent-to-own stereo system with about fifty-seven CDs, mostly funk and hip hop. Chango found a box of Hustlers and a Glock .40 that had fallen behind the box. For the hell of it, they took the dresser and the bunk beds from the kids' bedroom.

In the garage, there was a Toro lawn mower and, oddly, a snowblower. They took it all. As they were leaving,

Chango trotted back into the house and came out with a blender under his arm.

In and out in less than three hours. They were home for a late supper. The stuff went into the garage.

❧

Wednesday: three TVs, a tall iPod dock, a long couch painting, a washer and dryer, a new king-size bed still in plastic wrappers, whisky and rum, a minibike, and a set of skis.

Thursday: a navy peacoat, a mink stole (fake), six rings, another TV, another bed, a recliner chair and a matching couch in white leather, a shotgun and an ammo loading dock, a video porn collection, a framed swirl of blue tropical butterflies, golf clubs, a happening set of red cowboy boots.

Friday: aside from the usual swag—how sick were they of TV sets by now—they found an abandoned Mustang GT in the garage. Covered in dust, but sleek black. Chango wiped that baby down and Llaves hot-wired it for him and he drove back to San Diego in style.

It was a massive crime wave, and the only witnesses so far had been two kids and an ice cream man, and the ice cream man called, "Times are tough!" and Chango, into some Robin Hood hallucination, took him a thirty-two-inch flat screen and traded it for Sidewalk Sundaes for his boyz.

~

After a month of this, after dealing the goods out to fences and setting up a tent at the flea market, Chango and Junior were rolling in it. They paid their associates a fair salary, but their folding money was in fat rolls held together by rubber bands. Chango had the old repair bay in his house converted to a gym. NordicTrack, an elliptical, a Total Gym As Seen on TV, three sets of weights, and a Shake Weight that nobody wanted to touch because it looked like they were wanking when they were ripping their biceps.

"You don't make this kind of money selling dope to college girls," Chango said.

"No," Junior confessed. "Not lately."

He hadn't planned on selling pot to anyone. He had hoped to teach a good Acting 101 class. Maybe write a script or some poems. And there was a gal…well. Enough of that. He wasn't going there. Then he chided himself for thinking a cliché like "going there." No wonder he drank—it was the only way to shut his brain down. Fortunately, Chango had collected seven kinds of rum. Junior doctored his Coke Zero and lounged.

He had a cot in the corner of Chango's gas station. It was a little too close to Chango for comfort, and he had to put in his iPod buds to cancel out the old crow's snoring. But it was free, and the snacks and booze were good.

The Mustang sat out on the street. Junior kept telling

Chango it would get him busted, that it was too visible. But Chango was invincible. Chango told him, "Live, peewee. Ya gotta live!" There was a tin shower rigged up in one of the restrooms. Junior's stolen iPod port was blasting "Can't You Hear Me Knocking."

"Stones suck," said Chango, swallowing tequila. "Except for Keith. Keith's ba-a-ad."

Junior was thinking about the old times, how, when they'd gather at the bowling alley to play pinball, Chango would smoke those pestilential Dominos and force Junior to lose by putting the burning cherry on his knuckle every time he had to hit the bumpers.

"Fucker," he said.

"You got that right, homes."

"So, Chango—what's next?"

"We, um, steal a lot more shit."

"Shouldn't we cool it for a while? Let the heat die down?"

"Heat," Chango shrieked. "Did you actually say 'heat'? Haw! 'Heat,' he says. God DAMN." And then: "What heat?" He laughed out loud. "You seen cop one? We is invisible, homie. We just the trashman."

"I'm just being cautious," Junior said.

"I got it covered, peewee," Chango boasted. "Chango's got it all covered."

"Covered how?"

"Next stop," Chango announced, "Arizona! Don't nobody know us over there in 'Zoney!"

⁊

They should have never crossed the border. That's what Junior thought as he escaped. They didn't know anything about Arizona. Someone had seen them, he was pretty sure. It was probably at the motel outside of Phoenix. They'd probably been made there.

Whatever. It went bad right away. They drove around looking for abandoned houses, but in Arizona, how could you tell? All the yards were dirt, and the nice yards looked to them exactly like the bad yards. What was a weed and what was that xeriscaping desert shit?

In Casa Grande they felt like they were getting to it. A whole cul-de-sac had collected trash and a few tumbleweeds. Junior couldn't believe there were actual tumbleweeds out there. John Wayne–type stuff. They pulled in and actually rang the doorbells and got nothing. So Chango did his thing and went in the back and they were disappointed to find the first house completely vacant except for an abandoned Power Ranger action figure in the back bedroom and a melted bar of Dial in the bathroom.

The second house was full of fleas and sad, broken-ass welfare crap. Chango found a bag of lime and chili tortilla chips, and he munched these as he made his way to the third, and last, house. He went in. Score!

"I love the recession!" he shouted.

They drained the waterbed with a hose through the

bathroom window. Hey—a TV. These debt monsters really liked their giant screens. Massaging recliners. Mahogany tables and a big fiberglass saguaro cactus. "Arty," Chango said. Mirrors, clothes, a desktop computer and printer, a new microwave, two nice Dyson floor fans, a sectional couch in cowhide with brown and white color splotches. They even found a sewing machine.

It had taken too long, what with the long search and the three penetrations. After they loaded, pouring sweat except for "Mr. Petrucci," who sat in his a.c. so he'd look good in case any rubberneckers came along, it was four in the afternoon, and they were hitting rush hour on I-10.

The truck was a mile ahead. Junior liked to hang back and make believe he was driving on holiday. No crime. He was heading cross-country, doing a Kerouac. He was going back down to National City to find La Minnie, his sweet li'l ruca from the Bay Theater days. He should have never let her go. He hadn't gone to a single high school reunion, but his homeboy El Rubio told him La Minnie had asked about him. Divorced, of course. Who in America was not divorced? But still slim and cute and fine as hell. Junior knew his life would have been different if he'd done the right thing and stayed on W. 20th and courted that gal like she deserved, but he was hungry. Trapped like a wildcat in somebody's garage, and when the door cracked the slightest bit, he was gone.

These things were on his mind when the police lights and sirens went off behind him.

He had to give it to Chango—he played his string out right to the end.

The cops blasted past Junior's Buick and dogged the white U-Haul. Two cars. Llaves knew better than to try to run—the truck had a governor on the engine that kept it to a maximum speed of fifty-five. He puttered along, Junior back there shouting, "Shit! Shit! Shit!" Then he hit his blinker and slowly pulled over to the shoulder, the police cars insanely flashing and yowling. The associates were climbing out when Junior went by. He could see Chango's mouth already working.

He didn't know what to do. Should he keep going? Book and not look back?

He hit the next overpass and crossed over the freeway and sped back and crossed over again and rolled up behind the cop cars. He set his tie and pulled on his jacket with its name tag and even picked up his clipboard.

There were two cops—one Anglo and one Hispanic.

The associates stood in a loose group against the side of the truck. The cops turned and stared at Junior.

"Officers," he called. "I am Mr. Petrucci, from Bowden Federal in Detroit. Is there a problem?"

"Petrucci," said the Hispanic. "Is that Italian?"

"It is," said Junior.

"This dude," Chango announced, pointing at the cop, "is some kinda Tío Taco!"

"Shut it," the cop replied.

A Border Patrol truck pulled up behind the Buick.

"Sir?" said the cop. "I need to ask you to leave. You need to call your bank and have another team sent out to deliver these goods."

"Fuck!" shouted Chango.

"Is there a problem with . . . the load?" Junior asked.

"No, sir. This is strictly a ten-seventy stop."

"Ten-seventy?"

"SB ten-seventy. Immigration. We have reason to believe these gennermen are illegals."

The BP agent was eyeballing Chango.

Junior almost laughed.

"Why, I never!" he said.

Chango called, "He don't know shit. Fuckin' Petrucci. He's just a bean counter. Never did a good day's work in his life! That asshole don't even know us." He was playing to the crowd. "I worked every day! I paid my taxes! I-I-I served in Iraq!" he lied.

The cop held up two licenses in his fingers, as if he were making a tight peace sign or was about to smoke a cigarette. Llaves and Chango—Hugo didn't have a license.

"Do you have citizenship papers?" the BP man asked.

"I don't need no stinkin' papers! This is America!"

"Have they been searched?" BP asked.

"What are you, the Gestapo?" Chango smiled a little. He felt he had scored a major point. "I'm down and brown!" he hooted. "Racial profiling!" Etc.

"Not yet."

"I ain't being searched by nobody," Chango announced.

The BP man wagged his finger in Chango's face.

"I'll break that shit off and jam it up your ass," Chango said. "You think some wetback would say that?"

"We ran your license," the cop said. "Your address seems to be an abandoned gas station in San Diego."

The cops and the BP agent smirked at each other.

"Goddamned right I live in a gas station!" Chango bellowed. "My dad owned it!"

"Uh-huh."

The cop turned to Junior.

"I have to insist, Mr. Petrucci—you need to leave the scene. Now."

Junior stared at Chango and got into his Buick as the cops tossed the guys against the side of the panel truck and he saw, or thought he saw, just as he pulled into traffic, the Glock fall out of Chango's pocket and the cops draw and squat, shouting, and he hit the gas and was shaking with adrenaline or fear or both and didn't know what happened but he never slowed until he was in front of the old Esso station. He was stiff and sore and scared out of his mind. He ran into Chango's bedroom and tore open his Dopp kit and took his roll of cash. He thought for a minute and went out, locked the door, and slipped into the GT. The wires sparked when he touched them and the big engine gave a deep growl and shout, the glasspacks sounding sweet. He was going to go. Going to go. Just get out. Break the ties once and for all. Never look back. He was in the wind. Junior rubbed his face three or four times. He revved the big engine and put his foot on the pedal and stared. Night. Streetlights shining through the palm trees made octopus shadows in the street. Junior rolled down the window. He could smell Burger King. Two old women walked arm in arm, speaking Spanish. He could hear a sitcom through the open window of a bungalow above Chango's station. Junior knew if he headed down toward the old Ducommun warehouse, he could find La Minnie's mom's house. It was funky twenty years ago. With its geraniums. Minnie could be there. Or her family could tell him where she was. She used to like a sweet ride like this. Maybe she'd like to feel the wind in her hair. They could drive anywhere. He thought he could talk her into it, if he could find her. The way things had changed around town, the old house might not be there at all. Probably not. Probably gone with all the things he remembered and loved. But...he asked himself...what if it wasn't?

He shifted and moved steadily into the deeper dark.

Four

Carnations

They wore their best clothes and waited for the Old Man. Billy didn't own a suit, but he'd found a tie somewhere. He stood at the window, watching the Old Man water the garden.

His sister said, "What's he doing now?"

"Wait."

"We're going to be late."

"Just...wait."

She looked at her husband in the living room and shook her head. The Old Man, Mr. Iron Fist, loved drunken Billy the most. She sighed. Well, at least Billy'd cut his hair.

"He's getting dirty," she said.

Billy watched Pops shuffle in the dirt, mud on his brogans and dirt on his cuffs. That brown suit had to be fifty years old. But the fedora was stylin'. He smiled.

"I need a smoke," he said. His sister didn't smoke. "Start the car. I'll fetch him."

He stepped out of the gloom into a bright cube of light

and leaves and butterflies. Good stink of fresh mud. He lit up. Pops watered his apple tree.

"Getting late, Pops," he said.

The Old Man turned off the spigot.

"Sonny," he said. "We planted this tree the day you were born." He'd told this to Billy a thousand times.

Billy pulled out his handkerchief.

"You got mud on your shoes."

Pops braced himself on his kneeling son's shoulder as Billy cleaned his feet.

"Is it terrible, Billy?" he asked.

Billy led him around to the front. Pops paused and bent to the raised carnation beds. He plucked one and sniffed it.

"Mother's favorite," he said.

Billy tossed his smoke.

"It's not bad, Pops. Not too bad. She looks like she's asleep."

The car was waiting.

"Is it okay?" the Old Man asked. "I drop this flower in with her?"

Billy took his elbow. His arm felt like little sticks. The sidewalk was broken up out here. Uneven.

"It's okay, Pops. I promise."

Sis opened the door.

Pops tipped his hat to her and climbed in.

Five

Taped to the Sky

1. Keep Honking

Hey, boo," the waitress said. "What you know good?"

She was being folkloric. Hubbard was supposed to be charmed. But since the demise of The Previous Marriage, about five and a half days ago, he'd been sulky. He once read about a Sioux warrior named Cranky Man, and now he thought: *That's me*.

Lafayette, Louisiana, was as hot as the inside of your mouth.

"I don't know a damn thing," he replied.

"I don't know me too," she said, not taking to his Yankee-ass tone one bit. "But hey," she said. "What do I know. I'm just trailer trash from Butte La Rose."

"Is that bad?" Hubbard asked.

A little dark guy in a red gimme cap watched this, snorted, and nodded his head at her.

"She proud," he said. "She smacked you good."

She tossed him a smile and threw a hip in his direction.

Hubbard leaned an elbow on his little round table. It had gold foil ashtrays, with the corners sort of bent down to hold the smokes. Apparently, you could still smoke in bars in Acadiana. Hubbard didn't smoke.

The waitress raised an eyebrow at him.

"Beer," he said.

She let her gum answer as she turned away: *Pop! Pop! Pop!*

The guy in the cap said, "She just tryin' to be friendly." He was sipping chicory coffee—Hubbard could smell it across the gap between tables.

A stuffed gator stood on a platform in the middle of the restaurant, jaws agape, dust on its marble eyes.

Hubbard ignored Mr. Coffee and nodded when the waitress put his Abita beer down on a napkin and turned her back. It was so cold, some of the foam was ice slush. Oh yes. Oh yes. He took a long pull off the bottle. His eyes watered. She was a handsome woman, no doubt. Boo. He always thought southern women called you "sugar." He'd seen "boo" in James Lee Burke books, but this was the first time anybody had called him that.

Red Cap called him something different when he sidled his chair closer.

"Hey, asshole," he said.

Hubbard chewed another mouthful of slushy beer.

"You ain't from around here," Red Cap said.

"Passing through," Hubbard said.

"They teach you manners where you come from?"

"Nope. You?"

The dude sipped his coffee and chuckled.

"You funny, son," he said. He tipped his cap back and set his eyes in slits and regarded Hubbard some more.

Hubbard had spent his morning staring at bull gators and nutria rats in Lake Martin, between Lafayette and Breaux Bridge. It made him feel badass. This whole chunk of the map was written in poems and liquor bottle labels: Whiskey Bay, Catahoula, Atchafalaya. He'd bought a long gator fang from a Chittimacha Indian craftsman at the Festival Acadien and then danced a two-step with a blues singer named Lana. The fang hung on a black leather thong, nice and solid against his chest, making him feel wild and at large on the land. Not to be fucked with: Hubbard, Unbound.

He had the alligator hoodoo.

"You must be a comedian, yeah?" said the li'l dude.

Hubbard drained his beer, belched softly, and looked at him.

"Must be," he replied.

Red Cap turned in his chair. "See that sign out there?" he said. Hubbard squinted out the window. "What it say?"

"Poo-Yee," said Hubbard.

"No sir, it do not. It says Poo-Yi. 'Yi' as in 'eye,' see? An' you know what that means?"

Hubbard shook his head, thinking: *More beer.*

"That there is Cajun for 'North American ass-kicking establishment.' And y'all about to get a free lesson on how that works."

81

"Lately," said Hubbard, "I have been considering language to be the enemy."

Red Cap put down his cup.

"Is that right?"

The waitress dropped a coin in the juke: Beau Jocque and the Zydeco Hi-Rollers came on. "Can you really make it stink?" Beau Jocque demanded.

"My wife left me," Hubbard said. "I never understood a single thing she said."

Red Cap nodded sagely.

"Podnah," he said. "No wonder you in such a bad mood."

❧

Hubbard watched two Klansmen duke it out in Vidor, Texas. He could tell at least one of them was in the Klan because he had a purple KKK tattoo on his neck. The other fellow wore a stars'n'bars Confederate flag on his cap. Hubbard was deeply gratified to see he had a lightning bolt SS on his left bicep. He wanted these assholes to destroy each other.

He crunched Corn Nuts and watched the two trade blows and bear hug each other to carom off pickups and panel trucks in the parking lot. He held a banana Slurpee and was finally moved away by a scooting crowd of teens making a break for it when two new trucks sped into the lot. He pulled out and took a last glance at the mullet haircuts of the strangers flinging blood.

≈

America! Motel 8! Motel 6! The World's Largest Cross! The Lion's Den 24 Hour Adult Super Store—Buses Welcome!

He piloted his wife's Volvo west on I-10. Texas lasted for ten thousand miles till he found the San Antonio cutoff. He took a hotel room right at the split in the freeways. Fort Something. The vapor lamps in the parking lot turned his skin a vague shade of purple.

Huge stinkbugs swarmed the lot. They clanked out of the dark in black ranks and mounted each other everywhere around him. He was careful not to step on them because the many he'd already run over were wafting a bitter stench that went nicely with the toxic lights. A car passed by and the stinkbugs crackled like pecan shells. Hubbard held his breath.

He wrestled with the key card. Ground-floor room. He moved ecstatic stinkbug ménages aside with his foot. The door of the next unit opened, and a woman with a long T-shirt and shadowy eyes smiled out at him. He passed seven seconds daydreaming that she was a hooker and he'd spend $50 to show his ex something then pushed open his door and went inside and kicked it shut.

He tossed his duffel on one cardboard bed and threw his own carcass on the other. He thumbed through the channels on the TV—lots of Mexican telenovelas. On the bedside table, a Xeroxed menu from the Fort Something

Pizza Palace. *We Deliver to YOUR Room!* What the hell. He called and ordered spaghetti and beer. When it came, the Styrofoam box had a mound of mashed potatoes and gravy tucked in with the spaghetti.

Next door, his gal in the T-shirt was crying, "Kurt! Kurt! Oh my God, Kurt!"

Hubbard's ex had never once cried *Oh my God*.

At Las Cruces, he turned north. I-25. Big land, big sky, big spirits. Canned Heat on the deck. He rolled down the window and sang along: "I'm on the road again!" North! Albuquerque, Santa Fe, Pueblo, Denver. That's where he was going, by God.

He'd been eating his breakfast in El Paso, reading a paper with little transparent grease windows stained in the pages. He'd been in the old cemetery to gawk at John Wesley Hardin's grave. Murdering son of a bitch. He'd picked up a pebble from the pistoleer's grave and pocketed it. More hoodoo. And then he'd hopped over the wall and clocked on into the diner and it was chorizo and huevos and papitas and tortillas and Cholula and coffee, coffee, coffee. So what if she thought he was fat. He'd show her some fatness right here.

The paper had said there was a trailer park serial killer who slaughtered the innocent near Elephant Butte, around Truth or Consequences. And the killing fields were not far from the springs Cochise liked to bathe in. Why, hell—he was deep into some kind of strange Italian western. There were patterns moving across the sky, high, where small scallops of cloud shimmered like mother-of-pearl. He felt a part of the great becoming, the revelation of the West.

Up! To Billy the Kid's New Mexico. Up! To Colorado's Buffalo Bill and his grave! Boulder, where Tom Horn moldered beneath the grass! North—to the land of the Cheyenne and the Sioux and the Arapaho and the Crow! He was a killer on the road, he told himself, and when he got in the car to peel out of El Paso, he shoved The Doors into the CD slot and felt the power of the great silence.

Elephant Butte reflected red serial killer light onto its somnolent reservoir.

He took a detour out of Burque and headed west again, where the mesas were black and red and the rivers lay dead as bones under the sun. On the way to Rio Puerco he stopped in a cowboy bar. He thought he'd get drunk. He thought he'd get beat up. It would feel good. Indians looked at him when he walked in and laughed. He sat at a stool and sipped a Bud. A Navajo woman stepped up to him and asked him to dance on account of her old man's feet hurt too much from diabetes to get up off his chair. She came up to his chest, and she grinned at him the whole time. His dancing was apparently hilarious.

"You don't dance too much," she said.

"Not really."

"Pretty good," she said. "Don't feel bad." She laughed.

When they stepped outside to let the sweat dry, she said, "What are you?"

"Just a white boy."

"Oh," she said. "I thought you was a Leo."

❧

Up the Raton Pass, Hubbard was assaulted by Colorado. It was like some Maxfield Parrish painting, all electric blues and impossible neon clouds, ridiculous snowy peaks and bright yellow prairies. He pulled over and stared at it. By God, the world was full of color after all.

Then he cried.

❧

The car died in Wyoming.

Hubbard was angling northeast toward Fort Laramie. Not Laramie the town, which was a brief mirage on brown plains. But the old historical fort where the great chiefs and the great cavalrymen had parlayed. As far away from his stupid abandoned apartment in Cambridge as he could get. No goddamned tofu sausages in Fort Laramie!

The car got a little rough, then shouted at him and unleashed a stench not unlike the stinkbugs of far Texas. Then it shuddered and died. Hubbard wrestled the wheel as momentum rolled the Volvo into the weeds and a plume of smoke arose. Wind made its low song around him.

The key made the engine crunch and howl and whimper. Then nothing at all.

"Okay," he said, informing the universe he was ready for decisive action.

Got out. Walked around the car. Looked underneath. Didn't she take care of her car? It wasn't cheap. Used, yes—but not cheap. Cars were not his thing.

He got back in. Nothing. *Graveyard dead,* as cowboys said in books he'd read. He stared at the dials as if they would offer him an explanation.

The radio still worked, though. He turned the dial until he found Dr. Laura. She was of the opinion that a caller who fed his toddler Beano to keep her from farting was a weakling. He turned the radio off.

"Let's try again, shall we?" he announced.

Nothing happened.

✿

He sat on the hood, back to the windshield, reading Rilke. The heat of the dead engine felt good—Wyoming's brisk wind was frisking his body. His nipples were as hard as his John Wesley Hardin pebble. Nobody came down the road. He sipped water from a bottle with French writing on the label. He ate peanut M&M's. At least he had some protein.

Barbed wire twinkled like spiderwebs and dew. The sky went all the way up and over and down. He'd never seen so much sky. It looked like the little sage bushes on the horizon were buttons holding it to the ground.

He'd thought a rancher, a cowboy, somebody would drive by. So far, only crows. They seemed to be laughing at him.

Rilke said: *You are not too old, and it is not too late* ....

"Bullshit," he said.

That circling crow was unimpressed.

A white plastic bag danced in the nearest fence like Casper the Friendly Ghost.

"Wonderful," Hubbard noted.

⌘

Perhaps he would die out here. The Elements, he thought, as only a city boy would. But he was so betrayed, so alone. Suicide was not off the table, either. He pondered the amazing horror of his cold, cold body found here in the back of beyond. Pecked—pecked!—by crows. Rilke in his frozen hand.

Or starvation.

He was hungry.

He slid off the hood. Maybe she had some candy bars stashed in her glove compartment. She used to crack him up every time she announced that the best medication for PMS was chocolate. She called it her drug of choice. Twelve-stepper humor. Damn her.

The chairman of the Porter Square AA meeting had

been coming around their apartment. Hubbard writhed a little every time he remembered making this bastard his famous turkey chili. That Cantabrigian had twelve-stepped right into Mrs. Hubbard's bed. They called it a thirteenth step. He had taken a real inventory inside her knickers while Hubbard taught Beast Literature at Harvard Extension. Night school lectures in Apuleius and his use of the common ass in his fables.

Came home to find the Sting CDs gone. Odd. He thought she must have taken the boom box into the kitchen to wash the dishes. But the boom box was also gone. He looked in the bedroom—the bed was stripped. He said aloud, "If the tampons are gone, you have left me." The medicine cabinet was bare.

A gesture was called for.

He skulked over to the AA pimp's condo in Central Square and saw her Volvo parked outside. He had her spare key on his keychain. Popped the door and drove away, hit the ATM in Harvard Square, grabbed a duffel full of chinos and jeans and polo shirts and his Black Sabbath T at the apartment and headed down I-95 at an admirable clip.

"Grand theft auto!" he cried, half-giddy with himself.

New York: saw a biker with CHINGALING on his vest. Virginia: fog and a phantom roller-coaster beside the road. South Carolina: smokestack painted to look like a giant cigarette. Florida: he bought a cap with a gator on it that said FLORIDA YARD DOG.

In Alabama, he covered his wife's EASY DOES IT/LIVE AND LET LIVE bumper stickers with new ones. One of them said KEEP HONKING, I'M RELOADING! He had a pair of her panties with him. All the way across the South, he had told himself he could throw them out at any time.

⁂

A lone cloud sailed out of Colorado and evaporated in the Wyoming sky.

Hubbard popped open her glove box. Papers and whatnot tumbled out. Receipts, maps, registration, tampons, matches, ChapStick. He held a tampon and remembered. How she had dared him to insert one in her during her period. "Go on," she had taunted. "I won't break." How she'd stood with one foot on the toilet, and he had knelt there before her as if it were some ancient ritual, and he had tried to do it without somehow tearing secret woman-stuff in there. Thrilled and queasy in equal measure. It had seemed sacred at the time. He shook his head.

More clouds now, hanging above him as if they were pictures of clouds glued to a blue sheet of paper.

And that's when he found it. Her stash. A baggie full of pills and capsules. Pink ones. Blue ones. Red ones. A black one. White tabs with X's on them. AA, eh? Recovery, eh? Well, as the bluesmen said, well, well. Couples therapy. Sponsors. Al-Anon. And all the time she had this hidden in her car.

He fell back in the seat. He was done in. He laughed as he slapped the dash, his own head.

"Too much!" he cried.

After a while, it stopped being funny. Any of it. Cambridge. Harvard Extension. Who was he kidding? His day job was at a community college in Framingham. Harvard? One more ridiculous affectation. Everything in his life had ended up here, in the wasteland, with his engine burned to a crisp. How appropriate. This was the punch line of the cosmic joke. Hubbard the Absurd.

"To hell with it."

He tipped the bagful of pills into his mouth and washed it down with tepid French water.

He arranged himself on the hood. Then hopped down and trotted to the back of the car and found a scarf. He wrapped it jauntily around his neck and got back on the hood.

The crows lost interest and flew away.

Come, death.

Come.

2. Serenity Contract

Don Her Many Horses was on his way from Pine Ridge to Boulder. The crazy dudes of the Oyate organization at the college were throwing their yearly party. He never missed it. The theme this year was "Dances with Nerds." You were supposed to come as the biggest dweeb you could imagine.

Don had heard the term "big-time" in Rapid. A white biker had said it, and he liked it. He tried it now: *I'm going as a nerd, big-time.*

He was trying to quit smoking, and it wasn't going all that well. But he worked that Doublemint gum and drummed his fingers on the wheel, listening to Skynyrd. He did his best to ignore the Marlboro Red hard pack tucked into the visor.

He spied a tan Volvo on the right shoulder. Slowed down to take a look. A white guy asleep on the hood. What's the deal with white boys, anyway? Getting a tan out here?

Horses stared as he passed, his head clicking in small increments like the Terminator. About fifty yards down the road, he stopped. He watched in the rearview. That was just squirrely, that scene. Guy looked dead. His feet in high-tops splayed out, unmoving. His head slumped to the side, mouth open.

Horses told himself it wasn't any of his business. If some wasichu decided to get out here and croak—well, more power to him. Nothing good was going to come of getting involved.

He pulled over and parked. Checked his cell phone. No signal. But he already knew that. He put it in reverse and slowly backed up. Came even with the man and hit the window button.

"Hey," he said.

Nothing.

"Hey!"

Hubbard jumped, just a little.

"Hey! Wake up!"

Hubbard cracked his eyes open and cast around as if he were a scuba diver looking at a reef.

"Huh?" Hubbard said.

Don raised his hand.

"How," he said.

He loved saying that to white boys.

Hubbard focused his eyes.

"Some truck," he croaked.

"You all right?"

"Not exactly. All right. No."

Don nodded. Now he'd tore it—had to pull over. Had to make sure. Now this clown was going to be on his hands.

Hubbard looked at the cottonwood in the field.

"Car broke," he said.

Horses leaned over and stuck out his head to look at the Volvo. A thick braid tumbled down and hung there. "Let's take a look," Don said.

"Gee, could you?" Hubbard said.

Don Her Many Horses parked, put down his size-thirteen black cowboy boot.

Horses reached back into the truck and extracted a big black cavalry hat. It had a high crown and an ample brim, curved down over his eyebrows. Braided horsehair hatband, and a feather attached by some kind of thong.

"Nice hat," Hubbard said.

Horses walked past, saying nothing.

He rested his fists on his hips and observed the land-scape. He didn't seem to be in any particular hurry to rescue Hubbard. "Pronghorn," he said.

"Excuse me?" he shouted, barely maintaining.

"Pronghorn. Antelope. Right over there."

Hubbard squinted.

"I mean. Really! For Christ's sake!" he declared.

"What?" said Horses, thinking: *Oh, wonderful—white boy's crazy.*

Hubbard waved his hand as if to show Horses it was nothing.

"He's watching us," Horses said.

"As we are watching him." Hubbard smiled.

"You stretch out on the grass over there," Horses said, pointing with his chin. "He won't be able to stay away. He'll be so curious, he'll walk over to take a look."

"Do tell!" Hubbard enthused.

Horses said, "Watch this."

He took off his hat, waved it above his head. Suddenly, like a tawny ICBM, the little antelope sprang straight into the air. He pogoed away, bouncing along and casting disapproving glances back at them.

"Hey!" Hubbard cried.

"Yeah," Horses said. "Wish I had my rifle out."

"Pronghorn steak," said Horses. "Marinated in wild blueberries. That's good eatin'."

Screw it. He reached into the cab. Grabbed out his red

pack. Tapped out a smoke and hung it on his lip. "Smoke too much," he said, lighting up. "That's my Indian name." He rasped out a laugh, blew a stream of smoke at Hubbard. "Is that a bear claw?" he said.

Hubbard fingered his Chittimacha hoodoo on its thong. "Gaaatorrr. Tooothhh."

Horses fished out a chain from under his shirt.

"Grizzly," he said. "Clawwww."

Hubbard started weeping.

"What about the carrr?" he asked.

"The car?" said Horses. "It's a Volvo."

Hubbard just stared at him, eyes wet.

White guys, Horses thought. *They're just not that funny.*

While Don Her Many Horses tried the ignition and listened to its screech, Hubbard's pills kicked off like cheap Fourth of July fireworks. *Pop! Pow!* He flew off the hood and bounced around on the blacktop. Holy SHIT! The SUN! It was SO BRIGHT! He hopped around like a pronghorn at a rave. He was WHOLE. He was fully REALIZED. His high-tops were full of freakin' Flubber.

He pointed at Horses.

"Hey, Smoke Too Much!" he said. "They call you boo in Louisiana!"

"Oh yeah?"

"Cajun guys say Poo-Yi before they kick your ass!"

"That right."

"Boo!"

"Don't call me boo."

"Right!" Hubbard agreed. "Right, right, right? Who, me? Never. Not once. Never said boo in my life. I'm so amped."

"How's about that," muttered Horses, fiddling with knobs and the ignition. He got out. He stretched his back. "Your car's broke, for sure," he said.

"Not my car. Not really. I mean, I paid for it, sure. But it's hers. Still, I forked over the cash. Every cent! So it should be mine. Right? Did you see that crow? I own it now, I guess." He patted the Volvo. "My war pony!"

Horses crossed his arms and leaned against the car. Butt on the fender.

"You done paid every cent," he prodded.

"Right! Right-right. Every goddamned cent. Put her through *grad school*. How do you like that? Took her five years to get a stinking M.A.! Not to mention five years of couples therapy. Out of my pocket."

Horses listened as the whole sad story fell out.

"Smoke. Can I call you Smoke? Or do you prefer Mr. Too Much? Have you ever been in therapy? Did I ask you that? Whatever. Probably not. What do you do? Sweat lodge, am I right? Can we do a sweat lodge? As I was saying: therapy. That was the key, you see. The key to everything. Second only to recovery. Recover this!" he cried, grabbing his crotch.

"Whoa, now. You're getting skittish."

96

Hubbard sadly noted, "We'd even made out our serenity contract right before she left."

Horses looked bored with this happy horseshit.

Horses said, "Pop the hood latch."

Hubbard reached in and yanked the handle.

"Oh," he sighed, starting his long descent. "I suppose it was all inner-child-related."

Horses, bent into the maw of the car, said, "Inner child? You got an inner child?" He backed away. "What are you, pregnant?"

Then he laughed: *HAW!*

He walked around in a circle. Shook his head. *HAW!*

He raised his hands as if warding off a blow.

"Just funnin'," he said.

He reached into the engine compartment and pulled out the oil dipstick.

"Got a rag?" he said.

Hubbard reached in his pocket and pulled out his wife's panties.

Horses said, "Jesus Christ! Get rid of that!"

But Horses didn't need a rag after all. The dipstick was clean. Shiny. Devoid of oil. He whirled upon Hubbard and brandished it like a fencer approaching with a foil.

"Look at that," he said.

"What."

"No oil."

"So?"

"So—no oil."

"So what?"

"How far did you drive this rig?"

"I don't know. Boston to Florida. Texas. Here."

"Five thousand miles?" Horses cried. "Six? Are you kid-din' me?"

"It was a long journey," Hubbard declaimed. "Perhaps epic in scope. Still, it had to encompass my grief and sense of..."

"Bud," said Horses. "You drove six thousand miles and never checked your oil!"

Hubbard sneered.

"It's, like, a Volvo," he said. "Built to last. Duh."

Horses slammed the hood.

"I tell you what, kola," he said. "You done toasted this engine dead."

Hubbard, fully into his crash now, hung his head.

"Graveyard dead." He said.

What Don Her Many Horses did not want to do was to give this clown a ride to Colorado. He could either head on out, or stall long enough for somebody else to come along and take over the rescue operation. Ol' Mr. White Bread could hop in their car and be on his way.

Hubbard had started in on his recent domestic crisis again.

Horses said, "Hey, get over it."

"Excuse me—it's only been a week. Not even a week."

"Yeah, and a week ought to be long enough for you to get over it. Way I see it, you came out ahead."

"I. Was. Abandoned."

"You was set free. She set your spirit free, man. You ought to say a prayer for her."

Hubbard was silent.

"You owe her," Horses said.

He was looking south. He might have seen a windshield sparkle down there. You never knew. Deliverance seemed at hand.

He was dismayed to see the sparkle veer left and cut across the plain, trailing a vague dust cloud.

"Mind if I borrow your rifle?" Hubbard blurted.

Horses blinked at him.

"Your rifle. Can I use it? Just for a minute." Hubbard was riding back up the slope.

"What for?"

"I'm going to put my war pony out of its misery."

"You can't shoot a car. It's a felony or something."

"I already stole the damned thing."

This was getting interesting again. Horses had seen a lot of things, but he'd never seen a guy kill a car with a rifle.

"You know how to work a rifle?" he said.

"Sure. I got a marksmanship merit badge in the Scouts."

"He got a merit badge," Horses muttered.

He retrieved the rifle, loaded a few rounds from a box under the seat. Worked the lever.

He handed the rifle to Hubbard. "One thing," he said. "You even begin to aim that thirty-thirty at me, and I'm going to run you over."

He trotted to his rig, jumped in, locked the doors, and fired her up.

Hubbard sauntered to the Volvo and tried to control the weapon. It wobbled and drifted. He braced the rifle against his shoulder and popped off a round. A headlight exploded. The car barely rocked. He turned to Horses and grinned. Gave a big thumbs-up.

Crack!

Hole in the windshield.

Horses tooted the horn.

Crack!

✑

A rusted-out Datsun pickup with wire bundles and tools piled in the bed rolled up and sat there as Hubbard bushwhacked the Volvo.

The driver got out and tapped on Don's window.

"Yep?"

"Sir? What's the deal with this here?"

"Guy's killin' his wife's car."

"Dang."

"Yep."

"What she do, step out?"

"Ran, sounds like."

100

The driver called back to his bud, "Butch! Guy's killin' his wife's car."

"Sweet!" hollered Butch.

Crack!

The kid spit some chaw and said, "There goes the mirror."

"Yep."

Butch joined the party.

"How you figure in this?" he asked.

"I am an observer of life's many pleasures," Horses said.

"Shee-it."

"Sir?" the first waddy said. "You think I could get in a shot?"

Butch laughed.

"Sure," said Horses. "Why not." He fished out a few more rounds from his box. "Knock yourself out." The kid went over to Hubbard and shook his hand. Horses and Butch watched the rifle change hands. Hubbard slapped the kid on the shoulder.

"This'll be good," said Butch.

"Some days," Horses said, "it pays to get up."

"Ain't that the truth."

The kid worked the lever like the Rifleman and blasted the crap out of the car, shredding its tires and puncturing its flanks. Hubbard clapped and hopped around.

"Doin' the bunny hop," noted Butch.

The kid came back to Horses and handed him the rifle.

"Thank you, sir. 'Preciate it."

"Hey," said Horses. "You boys want to give this guy a ride?"

"Hell no," they said and hopped back in the Datsun and banged away.

When Horses looked back at Hubbard, he was passed out on the road, smiling at the sky.

Horses hung his rifle back on the rack. He slipped a Redbone CD into the player. He didn't like all that Carlos Nakai stuff—all them twiddly flutes. He liked guitars. He found Zep II and slotted it in next to Redbone. Going to be some Page and Plant kicking in before he hit the state line. Hubbard was flat on his back in the road like a fried egg. Horses rolled on down the lonesome highway.

He pulled over and said "Shit" and got out. He collected Hubbard, hefted him in a fireman's carry. His back hurt like hell. He piled Hubbard into the backseat. Dug a screwdriver out of his toolbox. Went back to the assassinated Volvo and unscrewed the license plates. He pulled the paperwork out of the glove compartment. Tossed it all in with Hubbard, who was snoring softly.

He drove on.

Had hours to go. He'd get there late, thanks to this little adventure. But wait till the Oyate guys found Hubbard passed out in the truck! Aw, hell. They'd think of all kinds of crazy shit to do to him.

It was a good day. Ten miles ahead, on the port side of the highway, there was a buffalo herd Horses liked to look at. And beyond that, to the starboard, a llama ranch amused him when he passed it. And ostriches. It was like a free zoo all of a sudden. And he knew the Rockies would appear out of the blue haze to his right. Bright and vivid on the horizon, looming as he veered nearer. Growing taller.

Horses remembered when he and the Brewer brothers had duct-taped Yellowhorse to the ceiling at his birthday party. Over to Porcupine. He'd shouted, "Get me down, you bastards!" Little skinny guy up there like he was floating. Horses couldn't stop laughing.

He looked at Hubbard in the rearview.

Yeah. Tape. Those Oyate boys, a hundred years ago they might have staked him out. Naked on an anthill. But tape. That was funny. Hubbard would wake up over their heads. Looking down at crazy Indians in nerd clothes dancing to B-52 records. Whooping. Smoke. Noise. Hubbard, unable to come down. Eyes like plates. Hubbard, caught up in the sky. Hubbard, learning to pray.

Six

Amapola

Here's the thing—I never took drugs in my life. Yeah, okay, I was the champion of my share of keggers. Me and The Pope. We were like, "Bring on the Corona and the Jäger!" Who wasn't? But I never even smoked the chronic, much less used the hard stuff. Until I met Pope's little sister. And when I met her, she was the drug, and I took her and I took her, and when I took her, I didn't care about anything. All the blood and all the bullets in the world could not penetrate that high.

The irony of Amapola and me was that I never would have gotten close to her if her family hadn't believed I was gay. It was easy for them to think a gringo kid with emo hair and eyeliner was "un joto." By the time they found out the truth, it was too late to do much about it. All they could do was put me to the test to see if I was a stand-up boy. It was either that or kill me.

You think I'm kidding.

At first, I didn't even know she existed. I was friends with Popo. We met in my senior year at "Camelback"—Cortez High. Alice Cooper's old school back in prehistory, our big claim to fame, though most of us had no idea who Alice Cooper was. VH1 was for grandmothers.

Still, you'd think the freak factor would remain high, right? But it was just another hot space full of Arizona Republicans and future CEOs and hopeless football jocks not yet aware they were going to be fat and bald, living in a duplex on the far side, drinking too much and paying alimony to the cheerleaders they never thought could weigh 298 pounds and smoke like a coal plant.

Not Popo. The Pope. For one thing, he had more money than God. Well, his dad and his aunt Cuca had all the money, but it drizzled upon him like the first rains of Christmas. He was always buying the beer, paying for gas and movie tickets and midnight runs to Taco Bell. "Good American food," he called it.

He'd transferred in during my senior year. He called it his exile. I spied him for the first time in English. We were struggling to stay awake during the endless literary conversations about A *Separate Peace*. He didn't say much about it. Just sat over there making sly eyes at the girls and laughing at the teacher's jokes. I'd never seen a Beaner kid with such long hair. He looked like some kind of Apache warrior, to tell you the truth. He had double loops in his left ear. He got Droogy sometimes and wore eyeliner under one eye. Those li'l born

again chicks went crazy for him when he was in devil-
boy mode.

And the day we connected, he was wearing a Cradle of
Filth T-shirt. He was staring at me. We locked eyes for a
second and he nodded once and we both started to laugh.
I was wearing a Fields of the Nephilim shirt. We were the
Pentagram Brothers that day, for sure. Everybody else must
have been thinking we were goth school shooters. I guess
it was a good thing Phoenix was too friggin' hot for black
trench coats.

Later, I was sitting outside the vice principal's office. Ray
Hulsebus, the nickelback on the football team, had called
me a faggot and we'd duked it out in the lunch court. Popo
was sitting on the wooden bench in the hall.

"Good fight," he said, nodding once.

I sat beside him.

"Wha'd you get busted for?" I asked.

He gestured at his shirt. It was originally black, but it
had been laundered so often it was gray. In a circle were the
purple letters *VU*. Above them, in stark white, one word:
HEROIN.

"Cool," I said. "Velvet Underground."

"My favorite song."

We slapped hands.

"The admin's not into classic rock," he noted. "Think
I'm...advocating substance abuse."

We laughed.

"You like *Berlin?*" he asked.

"Berlin? The old band?"

"Hell no! Lou Reed's best album, dude!"

They summoned him.

"I'll play it for ya," he said, and walked into the office.

And so it began.

Tía Cuca's house was the bomb. She was hooked up with some kind of Lebanese merchant. The whole place was cool floor tiles and suede couches. Their pool looked out on the city lights, and you could watch roadrunners on the deck cruising for rattlers at dusk. Honestly, I didn't know why Pope wasn't in some rich private school, but apparently his scholastic history was "spotty." I still don't know how he ended up at poor ol' Camelback, but I do know it must have taken a lot of maneuvering by his family. By the time we'd graduated, we were inseparable. He went to ASU. I didn't have that kind of money. I went to community college.

Pope's room was the coolest thing I'd ever seen. Tía Cuca had given him a detached single-car garage at the far end of the house. They'd put in a bathroom and made a bed loft on top of it. Pope had a king-size mattress up there, and a wall of CDs and the Bose iPod port, and everything was Wi-Fi'd to his laptop. There was a huge Bowie poster on the wall beside the door—in full Aladdin Sane glory, complete with the little shiny splash of come on his collarbone. It was so retro. My boy had satellite on a flat screen, and piles of DVDs around the slumpy little couch on the ground floor. I

didn't know why he was so crazy for the criminal stuff—
Scarface and *The Godfather.* I was so sick of Tony Mon-
tana and Michael Corleone! He had an Elvis clock—
you know the one—with the King's legs dancing back
and forth in place of a pendulum.

"Welcome," Pope said on that first visit, "to Disgrace-
land."

He turned me on to all that good classic stuff: Iggy,
T. Rex, Roxy Music. He wasn't really fond of new music,
except for the darkwave guys. Anyway, there we'd be,
blasting that glam as loud as possible, and it would get
late and I'd just fall asleep on his big bed with him. No
wonder they thought I was gay! Ha. We were drinking
Buds and reading *Chic* and *Hustler* mags we'd stolen from
his uncle Abdullah or whatever his name was. Aunt Cuca
once said, "Don't you ever go home?" But I told her,
"Nah—since the divorce, my mom's too busy to worry
about it."

One day I was puttering around his desk, looking at the
Alien figures and the Godzillas, scoping out the new copy
of *El Topo* he'd gotten by mail, checking his big crystals and
his antique dagger, when I saw the picture of Amapola behind his stack of textbooks. Yes, she was a kid. But what a
kid.

"Who's this?" I said.

He took the framed picture out of my hand and put it
back.

"Don't worry about who that is," he said.

Thanksgiving. Pope had planned a great big fiesta for all his homies and henchmen. He took the goth-gansta thing seriously, and he had actual "hit men" (he called them that) who did errands for him, carried out security at his concerts. He played guitar for the New Nouveau Nuevos—you might remember them. One of his "soldiers" was a big Irish kid who'd been booted off the football team, Andy the Tank. Andy appeared at our apartment with the invitation to the fiesta—we were to celebrate the Nuevos' upcoming year, and chart the course of the future. I was writing lyrics for Pope, cribbed from Roxy Music and Bowie's *Man Who Sold the World* album. The invite was printed out on rolled parchment and tied with a red ribbon. Pope had style.

I went over to Tía Cuca's early, and there she was— Amapola. She'd come up from Nogales for the fiesta, since Pope was by now refusing to go home for any reason. He wanted nothing to do with his dad, who had declared that only gay boys wore long hair or makeup or played in a band that wore feather boas and silver pants. Sang in English.

I was turning eighteen, and she was fifteen, almost sixteen. She was more pale than Popo. She had a frosting of freckles on her nose and cheeks, and her eyes were light brown, almost gold. Her hair was thick and straight and shone like some liquid. She was kind of shy, too, blushing when I talked to her.

The meal was righteous. They'd fixed a turkey in the Mexican style. It was stuffed not with bread or oysters, but with nuts, dried pineapple, dried papaya and mango slices, and raisins. Cuca and Amapola wore traditional Mexican dresses and, along with Cuca's cook, served us the courses as we sat like members of the Corleone family around the long dining room table. Pope had seated Andy the Tank beside Fuckin' Franc, the Nuevos' drummer. Some guy I didn't know but who apparently owned a Nine Inch Nails type synth studio in his garage sat beside Franc. I was granted the seat at the end of the table, across its length from Pope. Down the left side were the rest of the Nuevos—losers all.

I was trying to keep my roving eye hidden from The Pope. I didn't even have to guess what he'd do if he caught me checking her out. But she was so fine. It wasn't even my perpetual state of horniness. Yes it was. But it was more. She was like a song. Her small smiles, her graciousness. The way she swung her hair over her shoulder. The way she lowered her eyes and spoke softly...then gave you a wry look that cut sideways and made savage fun of everyone there. You just wanted to be a part of everything she was doing.

"Thank you," I said, every time she refilled my water glass or dropped fresh tortillas by my plate. Not much, it's true, but compared to The Tank or Fuckin' Franc, I was as suave as Cary Grant.

"You are so welcome," she'd say.

It started to feel like a dance. It's in the way you say it, not what you say. We were saying more to each other than Cuca or Pope could hear.

We were down to the cinnamon coffee and the red grape juice toasts. She stood behind me, resting her hands on the top of the chair. And Amapola put out one finger, where they couldn't see it, and ran her fingernail up and down between my shoulder blades.

Suddenly, supper was over, and we were all saying good night, and she had disappeared somewhere in the big house and never came back out.

Soon Christmas came, and Pope again refused to go home. I don't know how Cuca took it, having the sullen King Nouveau lurking in her converted garage. He had a kitsch aluminum tree in there. Blue ornaments. "Très Warhol." He sighed.

My mom had given me some cool stuff—a vintage Who T-shirt, things like that. Pope's dad had sent presents—running shoes, French sunglasses, a .22 target pistol. We snickered. I was way cooler than Poppa Popo. I had been down to Tucson, and I'd hit Zia Records and brought him some obscure 70s LPs: Captain Beyond, Curved Air, Amon Duul II, the Groundhogs. Pope got me a vintage turntable and the first four Frank Zappa LPs—how cool is that?

Pope wasn't a fool. He wasn't blind, either. He'd arranged a better gift for me than all that. He'd arranged for Amapola to come visit for a week. I found out later she had begged him.

"Keep it in your pants," he warned me. "I'm watching you."

Oh my God. I was flying. We went everywhere for those six days. The three of us, unfortunately. Pope took us to that fancy art deco hotel on the west side of Phoenix. That one with the crazy neon lights on the walls outside and the dark gourmet eatery on the ground-floor front corner. We went to movie matinees, never night movies. It took two movies to wangle a spot sitting next to her, getting Pope to relinquish the middle seat to keep us apart. But he knew it was a powerful movement between us, like continental drift. She kept leaning over to watch me instead of the movies. She'd laugh at everything I said. She lagged when we walked so I would walk near her. I was trying to keep my cool, not set off the Hermano Grande alarms. Suddenly he let me sit beside her. I could smell her. She was all clean hair and sweet skin. Our arms brushed on the armrest, and we let them linger, sweat against each other. Our skin forming a thin layer of wet between us, a little of her and a little of me mixing and forming something made of both of us. I was aching. I could have pole-vaulted right out of the theater.

She turned sixteen that week. At a three o'clock showing of *The Dark Knight*, she slipped her hand over the edge of the armrest and tangled her fingers in mine.

This time, when she left, Pope allowed us one minute alone in his garage room. I kissed her. It was awkward.

Delicious. Her hand went to my face and held it. She got in Cuca's car and cried as they drove away.

"You fucker," Popo said.

⁂

She didn't Facebook. Amapola didn't even email. Calling from Nogales was out of the question, even though her dad could have afforded it. When I asked Pope about his father's business, he told me they ran a duty-free import/export company based on each side of the border, in the two Nogaleses. Whatever. I just wanted to talk to Amapola. So I got stamps and envelopes. I was thinking, what is this, like, 1980 or something? But I wrote to her, and she wrote to me. I never thought about how instant messages or email couldn't hold perfume, or have lip prints on the paper. You could Skype naked images to each other all night long, but Amapola had me hooked with each new scent in the envelope. She put her hair in the envelopes. It was more powerful than anything I'd experienced before. Maybe it was voodoo.

At Easter, Cuca and her Lebanese hubby flew to St. Thomas for a holiday. Pope was gigging a lot, and he was seeing three of four strippers. I'll admit, he was hitting the sauce too much—he'd come home wasted and ricochet around the bathroom, banging into the fixtures like a pinball. I thought he'd break his neck on the toilet or the bathtub. He said the old man had been putting pressure on him—I had no idea how or what he wanted of Pope. He wanted the rock and roll foolishness to end, that's for sure.

"You have no idea!" Pope would say, tequila stink on his breath. "If you only knew what they were really like. You can't begin to guess." But, you know, all boys who wear eyeliner and pay for full-sleeve tats say the same thing. Don't nobody understand the troubles they've seen. I just thought Pope was caught up in being our Nikki Sixx. We were heading for fame, world tours. I thought.

Somehow, Pope managed to get Amapola there at the house for a few days. And there she was, all smiles. Dressed in black. Looking witchy and magical. Pope had a date with a girl named Demitasse. Can you believe that? Because she had small breasts or something. She danced at a high-end club that catered to men who knew words like "Demitasse." She had little silver vials full of "stardust," that's all I really knew. It all left Pope staggering and blind, and that was what I needed to find time alone with my beloved.

We tried to watch a movie, but our hands crept toward each other. Which led to kissing. And once we kissed, we no longer cared what was on the TV. I freed her nipple from the lace—it was pink and swollen, like a little candy. I thought it would be brown. What did I know about Mexican girls? She pushed me away when I got on top of her, and she moved my hand away gently when it slipped up her thigh.

Pope came home walking sideways. I had no idea what

time it was. I don't know how he got home. My pants were wet all down my left leg from hours of writhing with her. I knew I should be embarrassed but I didn't care. When Pope slurred, "My dad's in town," I didn't even pay attention. He went to Cuca's piano in the living room and tried to play some of "Tommy." Then there was a silence that grew long. We looked in there and he was asleep on the floor, under the piano.

"Shh," Amapola said. And "Wait here for me." She kissed my mouth, bit my lip.

When she came back down, she wore a nightgown that drifted around her legs and belly like fog. I knelt at her feet and ran my hands up her legs. She turned aside just as my hands crossed the midpoint of her thighs, and my palms slid up over her hip bones. She had taken off her panties. I put my mouth to her navel. I could smell her through the thin material.

"Do you love me?" she whispered, fingers tangled in my hair.

"Anything. You and me." I wasn't even thinking. "Us."

She yanked my hair.

"Do," she said. "You. Love me?"

Yank. It hurt.

"Yes!" I said. "Okay! Jesus! I love you!"

We went upstairs.

118

"Get up! Get up! Get the fuck up!" Popo was saying, ripping off the sheets. "Now! Now! Now!"

Amapola covered herself and rolled away with a small cry. Light was blasting through the windows. I thought he was going to beat my ass for sleeping with her. But he was in a panic.

"Get dressed. Dude—get dressed now!"

"What? What?"

"My dad."

He put his fists to his head.

"Oh shit. My dad!"

She started to cry.

I was in my white boxers in the middle of the room.

"Guys," I said. "Guys! Is there some trouble here?"

Amapola dragged the sheet off the bed and ran, wrapped, into the bathroom.

"You got no idea," Pope said. "Get dressed."

We were in the car in ten minutes. We sped out of the foothills and across town. Phoenix always looks empty to me when it's hot, like one of those sci-fi movies where all the people are dead and gone and some vampires or zombies are hiding in the vacant condos, waiting for night. The streets are too wide, and they reflect the heat like a Teflon cooking pan. Pigeons might explode into flame just flying across the street to escape the melting city bus. Pope was saying, "Just don't say nothing. Just show respect. It'll be okay. Right, sis?"

She was in the backseat.

"Don't talk back," she said. "Just listen. You can take it."

"Yeah," Pope said. "You can take it. You better take it. That's the only way he'll respect you."

My head was spinning.

Apparently, the old man had come to town to see Pope and meet me, but Pope, that asshole, had been so wasted he forgot. But it was worse than that. The old man had waited at a fancy restaurant. For both of us. You didn't keep Big Pop waiting.

You see, he had found my letters. He had rushed north to try to avert the inevitable. And now he was seething, they said, because Pope's maricón best friend wasn't queer at all, and was working his mojo on the sweet pea. My scalp still hurt from her savage hair-pulling. I looked back at her. Man, she was as fresh as a sea breeze. I started to smile.

"Ain't no joke," Pope announced.

"Look," he said. "It won't seem like it at first, but Pops will do anything for my sister. Anything. She controls him, man. So keep cool."

When we got there, Pope said, "The bistro." I had never seen it before, not really traveling in the circles that liked French food or ate at "bistros." Pops was standing outside. He was a slender man, balding. Clean-shaven. Only about five-seven. He wore aviator glasses, that kind that turn dark in the sun. They were deep gray over his eyes. He was standing with a Mexican in a soldier's uniform. The Mexican was over six feet tall and had a good gut on him.

The old man and the soldier stared at me. I wanted to laugh. That's it? I mean, really? A little skinny bald guy? I was invincible with love.

Poppa turned and entered the bistro without a word. Pope and Amapola followed, holding hands. The stout soldier dude just eyeballed me and walked in. I was left alone on the sidewalk. I followed.

They were already sitting. It was ice-cold. I tried not to stare at Amapola's nipples. But I noticed her pops looking at them. And then the soldier. Pops told her, "Tápate, cabrona." She had brought a little sweater with her, and now I knew why. She primly draped herself.

"Dad...," said Pope.

"Shut it," his father said.

The eyeglasses had become only half-dark. You could almost see his eyes.

A waiter delivered a clear drink.

"Martini, sir," he said.

It was only about eleven in the morning.

Big Poppa said, "I came to town last night to see you." He sipped his drink. "I come here, to this restaurant. Is my favorite. Is comida francés, understand? Quality." Another sip. He looked at the soldier—the soldier nodded. "I invite you." He pointed at Pope. Then at her. Then at me. "You, you, and you. Right here." He drained the martini and snapped his fingers at the waiter. "An' I sit here an' wait."

The waiter hurried over and took the glass and scurried away.

"Me an' my brother, Arnulfo."

He put his hand on the soldier's arm.

"We wait for you."

Popo said, "Dad..."

"Cállate el osico, chingado," his father growled from deep in his chest so only I could hear him. He turned his head to me and smiled. He looked like a moray eel in a tank. Another martini landed before him.

He sipped. "I wait for you, but you don't care. No! Don't say nothing. Listen. I wait, and you no show up here to my fancy dinner. Is okay. I don't care." He waved his hand. "I have my li'l drink, and I don't care." He toasted me. He seemed like he was coiled, steel springs inside his gut. My skin was crawling and I didn't even know why.

"I wait for you," he said. "Captain Arnulfo, he wait. You don't care, right? Is okay! I'm happy. I got my martinis, I don't give a shit."

He smiled, and I was pretty certain he did give a shit.

He pulled a long cigar out of his inner pocket. He bit the end off and spit it on the table. He put it in his mouth. Arnulfo took out a gold lighter and struck a blue flame.

The waiter rushed over and murmured, "I'm sorry, sir, but this is a nonsmoking restaurant. You'll have to take it outside."

The old man didn't even look at him—just stared at me through those gray lenses.

"Is hot outside," he said. "Right, gringo? Too hot?" I nodded—I didn't know what to say.

"I must insist," the waiter said.

"Bring the chef," the old man said.

"Excuse me?"

"Get the chef out here. Now."

The waiter brought out the chef, who bent down to the old man. Whispers. No drama. But the two men hurried away and the waiter came back with an ashtray. Arnulfo lit Poppa's cigar.

He blew smoke at me and said, "Why you do this violence to me?"

"I—" I said.

"Shut up."

He snapped his fingers again, and food and more martinis arrived. I stared at my plate. Snails in garlic butter. I couldn't eat, couldn't even sip the water. Smoke drifted to me. I could feel the gray lenses focused on me. Pope, that chickenshit, just ate and never looked up. Amapola sipped iced coffee and stared out the window.

After forty minutes of this nightmare, Poppa pushed his plate away.

"Oye," he said, "tú."

I looked up.

"Why you wan' fock my baby daughter?"

☙

Sure, I trembled for a while after that. I got it, I really did. But did good sense overtake me? What do you think? I was full-on into the Romeo and Juliet thing, and she was even worse. Parents—you want to ensure your daughters marry young? Forbid them from seeing their boyfriends. Just try it.

"Uncle Arnie," as big, dark Captain Arnulfo was called in Cuca's house, started hanging around. A lot. I wasn't, like, stupid. I could tell what was what—he was sussing me out. He sidled up to me and said dumb things like "You like the sexy?" Pope and I laughed all night after Uncle Arnie made his appearances. "You make the sexy-sexy in cars?" What a dork, we thought.

My beloved showered me with letters. I had no way of knowing if my own letters got to her or not, but she soon found an Internet café in Nogales and sent me cyber-love. Popo was drying up a little, not quite what you'd call sober, but occasionally actually on the earth, and he started calling me "McLovin'." I think it was his way of trying to tone it down. "Bring it down a notch, homeboy," he'd say when I waxed overly poetic about his sister.

One Saturday I was chatting online with Amapola. That's all I did on Saturday afternoons. No TV, no cruising in the car, no movies or pool time. I fixed a huge vat of sun tea and hit my laptop and talked to her. Mom was at work—she was always at work or out doing lame shit like bowling. It was just me, the computer, my distant girlie, and the cat rubbing against my leg. I'll confess to you— don't laugh—I cried at night thinking about her.

Pope said I was whipped. I'd be like, that's no way to talk about your sister. She's better than all of you people! He'd just look at me out of those squinty Apache eyes. "Maybe," he'd drawl. "Maybe…" And I was just thinking about all that on Saturday, going crazier and crazier with the desire to see her sweet face every morning, her hair on my skin every night, mad in love with her, and I was IM-ing her that she should just book. Run away. She was almost seventeen already. She could catch a bus and be in Phoenix in a few hours and we'd jump on I-10 and drive to Cali. I didn't know what I imagined—just us, in love, on a beach. And suddenly, the laptop crashed. Just gone— a black screen before Amapola could answer me. I booted back up, not thinking much about it, but she was gone. Completely. I couldn't even find her account in my history. That was weird, I thought. I figured it for some sort of computer glitch, cursed and kicked stuff, then I grabbed a shower and rolled.

When I cruised over to Aunt Cuca's, everyone was gone. Only Uncle Arnie was left, sitting in the living room in his uniform, sipping coffee.

"They all go on vacation," he said. "Just you and me."

Vacation? Pope hadn't said anything about vacations. Not that he was what my English profs would call a reliable narrator.

Arnie gestured for me to sit. I stood there.

"Coffee?" he offered.

"No thanks."

"Sit!"

I sat.

I never really knew what the F Arnie was mumbling, to tell you the truth. His accent was all bandido. I often just nodded and smiled, hoping not to offend the dude, lest he freak out and bust caps in me.

"You love Amapola," he said. It wasn't a question. He smiled sadly, put his hand on my knee.

"Yes, sir," I said.

He nodded. Sighed.

"Love," he said. "Is good, love."

"Yes, sir."

"You not going away, right?"

I shook my head.

"No way."

"So. What this means? You marry the girl?"

Whoa. Marry? I...guess...I was going to marry her. Someday.

Sure, you think about it. But to say it out loud. That was hard. But I felt like some kind of breakthrough was happening here. The older generation had sent an emissary; perhaps they were warming up to me.

"I believe," I said, mustering some balls, "yes. I will marry Amapola. Someday. You know."

He shrugged, sadly. I thought that was a little odd, frankly. He held up a finger and busted out a cell phone, hit the speed button, and muttered in Spanish. Snapped it shut. Sipped his coffee.

"We have big family reunion tomorrow. You come. Okay? I'll fix up all with Amapola's papá. You see. Yes?"

I smiled at him, not believing this turn of events.

"Big Mexican rancho. Horses. Good food. Mariachis." He laughed. "And love! Two kids in love!"

We slapped hands. We smiled and chuckled. I had some coffee.

"I pick you up here at seven in the morning," he said. "Don't be late."

❧

The morning desert was purple and orange. The air was almost cool. Arnie had a Styrofoam cooler loaded with Dr. Peppers and Cokes. He drove a bitchin' S-Class Benz. It smelled like leather and aftershave. He kept the satellite tuned to BBC Radio 1. "You like the crazy maricón music, right?" he asked.

"...ah...right."

It was more like flying than driving, and when he sped past Arivaca, I wasn't all that concerned. I figured we were going to Nogales, Arizona. But we slid through that little dry town like a shark and crossed into Mex without hardly slowing down. At the border, he just raised a finger off the steering wheel and motored along, saying, "You going to like this."

And then we were through Nogales, Mexico, too. Black and tan desert. Saguaros and freaky burned-looking cactuses. I'm not an ecologist—I don't know what that stuff was. It was spiky.

We took a long dirt side road. I was craning around, looking at the bad black mountains around us.

We came out in a big valley. There was an airfield of some sort there. Mexican army stuff—trucks, Humvees. Three of four hangars or warehouses. Some shiny Cadillacs and SUVs scattered around.

"You going to like this," Arnie said. "It's a surprise."

There was Big Poppa Popo, the old man himself. He was standing with his hands on his hips. With a tall American. Those dark gray lenses turned toward us. We parked. We got out.

"What's going on?" I asked.

"Shut up," said Arnie.

"Where's the rancho?" I asked.

The American burst out laughing.

"Jesus, kid!" he shouted. He turned to the old man. "He really is a dumb shit."

The American walked away without introducing himself and got in a white SUV. He slammed the door and drove into the desert, back the way we had come. We stood there watching him go. I'm not going to lie—I was getting scared.

"You gonna marry Amapola?" the old man asked me.

"One day. Look, I don't know what you guys are doing here, but—"

He turned from me and gestured toward a helicopter sitting on the field.

"Look at that," he said. "Huey. Old stuff, from your Vietnam. Now the Mexican air force use it to fight las drogas." He turned to me. "You use las drogas?"

"No! Never."

They laughed.

"Sure, sure," the old man said.

"Ask Amapola!" I cried. "She'll tell you!"

"She already tell me everything," he said.

Arnie put his arm around my shoulders.

"Come," he said, and started walking toward the helicopter. I resisted for a moment, but the various Mexican soldiers standing around were suddenly really focused and not slouching and were walking along all around us.

"What is this?" I said.

"You know what I do?" the old man asked.

"Business?" I said. My mind was blanking out, I was so scared.

"Business." He nodded. "Good answer."

We came under the blades of the big helicopter. I'd never been near one in my life. It scared the crap out of me. The Mexican pilots looked out their side windows at me. The old man patted the side of the machine.

"President Bush!" he said. "DEA!"

I looked at Arnie. He smiled, nodded at me. "Fight the drogas," he said.

The engines whined and chuffed and the rotor started to turn.

"Is very secret what we do," said the old man. "But

you take a ride and see. Is my special treat. You go with Arnulfo."

"Come with me," Arnie said.

"You go up and see, then we talk about love."

The old man hurried away, and it was just me and Arnie and the soldiers with their black M16s.

"After you," Arnie said.

He pulled on a helmet. Then we took off. It was rough as hell. I felt like I was being punched in the ass and lower back when the engines really kicked in. And when we rose, my guts dropped out through my feet. I closed my eyes and gripped the webbing Arnie had fastened around my waist. "Holy God!" I shouted. It was worse when we banked— the side doors were wide open, and I screamed like a girl, sure I was falling out. The Mexicans laughed and shook their heads, but I didn't care.

Arnie was standing in the door. He unhooked a big gun from where it had been strapped with its barrel pointed up. He dangled it in the door on cords. He leaned toward me and shouted, "Sixty caliber! Hung on double bungees!" He slammed a magazine into the thing and pulled levers and snapped snappers. He leaned down to me again and shouted, "Feel the vibration? You lay on the floor, it makes you come!"

I thought I heard him wrong.

We were beating out of the desert and into low hills. I could see our shadow below us, fluttering like a giant bug on the rises and over the bushes. The seat kicked up and we were rising.

Arnulfo took a pistol from his belt and pointed down.

"Amapola," he said.

I looked around for her, stupidly. But then I saw what was below us, in a watered valley. Orange flowers. Amapola. Poppies.

"This is what we do," Arnulfo said.

He raised his pistol and shot three rounds out the door and laughed. I put my hands over my ears.

"You're DEA?" I cried.

He popped off another round.

"Is competition," he said. "We do business."

Oh my God.

He fell against me and was shouting in my ear and there was nowhere I could go. "You want Amapola? You want to marry my sobrina? Just like that? Really? Pendejo." He grabbed my shirt. "Can you fly, gringo? Can you fly?" I was shaking. I was trying to shrink away from him, but I could not. I was trapped in my seat. His breath stank, and his lips were at my ear like hers might have been and he was screaming, "Can you fly, chingado? Because you got a choice! You fly, or you do what we do."

I kept shouting, "What? What?" It was like one of those dreams where nothing makes sense. "What?"

"You do what we do, I let you live, cabrón."

131

"What?" I was screaming too.

"I let you live. Or you fly. Decide."

"I don't want to die!" I yelled. I was close to wetting my pants. The Huey was nose-down and sweeping in a circle. I could see people below us, running. A few small huts. Horses or mules. A pickup started to speed out of the big poppy field. Arnulfo talked into his mike and the helicopter hove after it. He took up the .60 caliber and braced himself. I put my fingers in my ears. And he ripped a long stream of bullets out the door. It was the loudest thing I'd ever heard. Louder than the loudest thing you can imagine. So loud your insides jump, but it all becomes an endless rip of noise, like thunder is inside your bladder and your teeth hurt from gritting against it.

The truck just tattered, if metal can tatter. The roof of the cab blew apart and the smoking ruin of the truck spun away below us and vanished in dust and smoke and steam.

I was crying.

"Be a man!" Arnulfo yelled.

We were hovering. The crew members were all turned toward me, staring.

Arnie unsnapped my seat webbing.

"Choose," he said.

"I want to live."

"Choose."

You know how it goes in the movies. How the hero kicks the bad guy out the door and sprays the Mexican crew with the .60 and survives a crash landing. But that's not real life. That doesn't even cross your mind. Not even close. No, you get up on terribly shaky legs, so shaky you might pitch out the open door all by yourself and discover that you cannot, in fact, fly. You say, "What do I do?" And the door gunner grabs you and shoves you up to the hot gun. The ground is wobbling far below you, and you can see the Indian workers down there. Six men and a woman. And they're running. You're praying and begging God to get you out of this somehow and you're thinking of your beautiful lover and you tell yourself you don't know how you got here and the door gunner comes up behind you now, he slams himself against your ass, and he says, "Hold it, lean into it. It's gonna kick, okay? Finger on the trigger. I got you." And you brace the .60 and you try to close your eyes and you pray you miss them and you're saying *Amapola, Amapola* over and over in your mind, and the gunner is hard against you, he's erect and pressing it into your buttocks and he shouts, "For love!" and you squeeze the trigger.

Seven

Mr. Mendoza's Paintbrush

When I remember my village, I remember the color green. A green that is rich, perhaps too rich, and almost bubbling with humidity and the smell of mangos. I remember heat, the sweet sweat of young girls that collected on my upper lip as we kissed behind the dance stand in the town square. I remember days of nothing and rainstorms, dreaming of making love while walking around the plazuela, admiring Mr. Mendoza's portraits of the mayor and the police chief, and saying dashing things to the girls. They, of course, walked in the opposite direction, followed closely by their unsympathetic aunts, which was only decent. Looking back, I wonder if perhaps saying those dashing things was better than making love.

Mr. Mendoza wielded his paintbrush there for thirty years. I can still remember the old women muttering bad things about him on their way to market. This was nothing extraordinary. The old women muttered bad things about most of us at one time or another, especially when they were on their way to market at dawn, double file, dark shawls pulled tight around their faces, to buy pots of warm milk with the cows' hairs still floating in them. Not until later in the day, after their cups of coffee with a bit of this hairy milk (strained through an old cloth) and many spoonfuls of sugar, would they finally begin to concede the better points of the populace. Except for Mr. Mendoza.

Mr. Mendoza had taken the controversial position that he was the Graffiti King of All Mexico. But we didn't want a graffiti king.

My village is named El Rosario. Perhaps being named after a rosary was what gave us our sense of importance, a sense that we from Rosario were blessed among people, allowed certain dispensations. The name itself came from a Spanish monk—or was it a Spanish soldier—named Bonifacio Rojas, who broke his rosary. The beads cascaded over the ground. Kneeling to pick them up, he said a brief prayer asking the Good Lord to direct him to the beads. Like all good Catholics, he offered the Lord a deal: If you give me my beads back, I will give you a cathedral on the spot. The Good Lord sent down St. Elmo's fire, and directly beneath that, the beads. Bonifacio got a taste of the Lord's wit, however, when he found an endless river of silver directly beneath the beads. It happened in 1655, the third of August. A Saturday.

The church was built, obliterating the ruins of an Indian settlement, and Rosario became the center of Chametla province. For some reason, the monks who followed Bonifacio took to burying each other in the cathedral's thick adobe walls. Some mysterious element in our soil mummifies monks, and they stood in the walls for five hundred years. Now that the walls are crumbling, though, monks pop out with dry grins about once a year.

When I was young, there was a two-year lull in the gradual revelation of monks. We were certain that the hidden fathers had all been expelled from the walls. A thunderclap proved us wrong.

Our rainy season begins on the sixth of June, without fail. That year, however, the rain was a day late, and the resulting thunderclap that announced the storm was so explosive, windows cracked on our street. Burros on the outskirts burst open their stalls and charged through town throwing kicks right and left. People near the river swore their chickens laid square eggs. The immense frightfulness of this celestial apocalypse was blamed years afterward for gout, diarrhea, birthmarks, drunkenness, and those mysterious female aches nobody could define but everyone called *dolencias*. There was one other victim of the thunderclap—the remaining church tower split apart and dropped a fat slab of clay into the road. In the morning, my cousin Jaime and I were thrilled to find a mummified hand rising from the rubble, one saffron finger aimed at the sky.

"An evangelist," I said.

"Even in death," he said.

We moved around the pile to see the rest of him. We

were startled to find a message painted on the monk's chest:

HOW DO YOU LIKE ME NOW?
DEFLATED! DEFLATE
YOUR POMP OR FLOAT AWAY!

"Mr. Mendoza," I said.
"He's everywhere," Jaime said.

ʆ

On the road that runs north from Escuinapa to my village, there is a sign that says:

ROSARIO POP. 8000

Below that, in Mr. Mendoza's meticulous scrawl:

NO INTELLIGENT LIFE FOR 100 KILOMETERS

There is a very tall bridge at the edge of town that spans the Baluarte River. My cousin Jaime told me that once a young man sat on the railing trading friendly insults with his friends. His sweetheart was a gentle girl from a nice family. She was wearing a white blouse that day. She ran up to him to give him a hug, but instead she knocked him from his perch, and he fell, arms and legs thrown open to the wind. They had to hold her back, or she would have joined him. He called her name all the way down, like a lost love letter spinning in the wind. No one ever found the body. They say she left town and married. She had seven sons, and each one was named after her dead lover. Her husband left her. Near this fatal spot on the bridge, Mr. Mendoza suggested that we

UPEND HYPOCRITES TODAY

Across town from the bridge, there is a gray whorehouse next to the cemetery. This allows the good citizens of the village to avoid the subjects of death and sex at the same time. On the wall facing the street, the message:

TURN YOUR PRIDE ON ITS BACK
AND COUNT ITS WIGGLY FEET

On the stone wall that grows out of the cobble street in front of the cemetery, a new announcement appeared:

MENDOZA NEVER SLEPT HERE

What the hell did he mean by that? There was much debate in our bars over that one. Did Mr. Mendoza mean this literally, that he had never napped between the crumbling stones? Well, so what? Who would?

No, others argued. He meant it philosophically—that

141

Mr. Mendoza was claiming he'd never die. This was most infuriating. Police Chief Reyes wanted to know, "Who does Mr. Mendoza think he is?"

Mr. Mendoza, skulking outside the door, called in, "I'll tell you! I'm Mendoza, that's who! But who—or what—are you!"

His feet could be heard trotting away in the dark.

Mr. Mendoza never wrote obscenities. He was far too moral for that. In fact, he had been known to graffito malefactors as though they were road signs. Once, Mr. Mendoza's epochal paintbrush fell on me.

It was in the summer, in the month of August, Bonifacio's month. August is hot in Rosario, so hot that snapping turtles have been cooked by sitting in shallow water. Their green flesh turns gray and peels away to float down the eternal Baluarte. I always intended to follow the Baluarte downstream, for it carried hundreds of interesting items during flood times, and I was certain that somewhere farther down there was a resting place for it all. The river seemed, at times, to be on a mad shopping spree, taking from the land anything it fancied. Mundane things such as trees, chickens, cows shot past regularly. But marvelous things floated there too: a green DeSoto with its lights on, a washing machine with a religious statue in it as though the saint were piloting a circular boat, a blond wig that looked like a giant squid, a mysterious star-shaped object barely visible under the surface.

The Baluarte held me in its sway. I swam in it, fished and

caught turtles in it. I dreamed of the distant bend in the river where I could find all these floating things collected in neat stacks, and perhaps a galleon full of rubies, and perhaps a damp yet lovely fifteen-year-old girl in a red dress to rescue, and all of it speckled with little gray flecks of turtle skin.

Sadly for me, I found out that the river only led to swamps that oozed out to the sea. All those treasures were lost forever and I had to seek a new kind of magic from my river. Which is precisely where Mr. Mendoza found me, on the banks of the post-magical Baluarte, lying in the mud with Jaime, gazing through a stand of reeds at some new magic.

Girls. We had discovered girls. And a group of these recently discovered creatures was going from the preparatory school's sweltering rooms to the river for a bath. They had their spot, a shielded kink in the river that had a natural screen of trees and reeds and a sloping sandy bank. Jaime and I knew that we were about to make one of the greatest discoveries in recent history, and we'd be able to report to the men what we'd found out.

"Wait until they hear about this," I whispered.

"It's a new world," he replied.

We inserted ourselves in the reeds, ignoring the mud soaking our knees. We could barely contain our longing and emotion. When the girls began to strip off their uniforms, revealing slips, then bright white bras and big cotton underpants, I thought I would sob.

"I can't," I said, "believe it."

"History in the making," he said.

The bras came off. They dove in.

"Before us is everything we've always wanted," I said.

"Life itself," he said.

"Oh you beautiful girls!" I whispered.

"Oh you girls of my dreams!" said he, and Mr. Mendoza's claws sank into our shoulders.

We were dragged a hundred meters upriver, all the while being berated without mercy. "Tartars!" he shouted. "Peeping Toms! Flesh chasers! Disrespecters of privacy!"

I would have laughed if I had not seen Mr. Mendoza's awful paintbrush standing in a freshly opened can of black paint.

"Uh-oh," I said.

"We're finished," said Jaime.

Mr. Mendoza threw me down and sat on me. The man was skinny. He was bony, yet I could not buck him off. I bounced like one of those thunderstruck burros, and he rode me with aplomb.

He attacked Jaime's face, painting:

I AM FILTHY

He then peeled off Jaime's shirt and adorned his chest with:

I LIVE FOR SEX AND THRILLS

He then yanked off Jaime's pants and decorated his rump with:

KICK ME HARD

I was next.
On my face:

PERVERT

On my chest:

MOTHER IS BLUE WITH SHAME

On my rump:

THIS IS WHAT I AM

I suddenly realized that the girls from the river had quickly dressed themselves and were giggling at me as I jumped around naked. It was unfair! Then, to make matters worse, Mr. Mendoza proceeded to chase us through town while people laughed at us and called out embarrassing weights and measures.

We plotted our revenge for two weeks, then forgot about it. In fact, Jaime's *I LIVE FOR SEX* made him somewhat of a celebrity, that phrase being very macho. He was often known after that day as "El Sexi." In fact, years later, he would marry one of the very girls we had been spying on.

There was only one satisfaction for me in the whole sad affair: the utter disappearance of the street of my naked humiliation.

*

Years after Bonifacio built his church in Rosario, and after he had died and was safely tucked away in the church walls (until 1958, when he fell out on my uncle Jorge), the mines got established as a going concern. Each vein of silver seemed to lead to another. The whole area was a network of ore-bearing arteries.

Tunnels were dug and forgotten as each vein played out and forked off. Often, miners would break through a wall of rock only to find themselves in an abandoned mineshaft going in the other direction. Sometimes they'd find skeletons. Once they swore they'd encountered a giant spider that caught bats in its vast web. Many of these mine shafts filled with seepage from the river, forming underground lagoons that had fat white frogs in them and an albino alligator that floated in the dark water waiting for helpless miners to stumble and fall in.

Some of these tunnels snaked under the village. At times, with a *whump*, sections of Rosario vanished. Happily, I watched the street Mr. Mendoza had chased me down drop from sight after a quick shudder. A store and six houses dropped as one. I was particularly glad to see Antonia Barrego vanish with a startled look while sitting on her porch yelling insults at me. Her voice rose to a horrified screech that echoed loudly underground as she went down. When she was finally pulled out (by block and tackle, the sow), she was all wrinkled from the smelly water, and her hair was alive with squirming white polly-wogs.

After the street vanished, my view of El Yauco was clear and unobstructed. El Yauco is the mountain that stands across the Baluarte from Rosario. The top of it looks like the profile of John F. Kennedy in repose. The only flaw in this geographic wonder is that the nose is up-side down.

Once, when Jaime and I had painfully struggled to the summit to investigate the nose, we found this message:

MOTHER NATURE HAS NO RESPECT FOR YANQUI
PRESIDENTS EITHER!

Nothing, though, could prepare us for the furor over his next series of messages. It began with a piglet running through town one Sunday. On its flanks, in perfect cursive script:

MENDOZA GOES TO HEAVEN ON TUESDAY

On a fence:

MENDOZA ESCAPES THIS HELLHOLE

On my father's car:

I'VE HAD ENOUGH!
I'M LEAVING!

Rumors flew. For some reason, the arguments were fierce, impassioned, and there were any number of fist-fights over Mr. Mendoza's latest. Was he going to kill himself? Was he dying? Was he to be abducted by flying saucers or carried aloft by angels? The people who were convinced the old *MENDOZA NEVER SLEPT HERE* was a strictly philosophical text were convinced he was indeed going to commit suicide. There was a secret that showed in their faces—they were actually hoping he'd kill himself, just to maintain the status quo, just to ensure that everyone died.

Rumors about Mendoza's health washed through town: cancer, madness (well, we all knew that), demonic possession, the evil eye, a black magic curse that included love potions and slow-acting poisons, and the dreaded syphilis. Some of the local smart alecks called the whorehouse "Heaven," but Mr. Mendoza was far too moral to even go in there, much less advertise it all over town.

I worked in Crispin's bar, taking orders and carrying

trays of beer bottles. I heard every theory. The syphilis one really appealed to me because young fellows always love the gruesome and lurid, and it sounded so nasty, having to do, as it did, with the nether regions.

"Syphilis makes it fall off," Jaime explained.

I didn't want him to know I wasn't sure which "it" fell off, if it was *it,* or some other "it." To be macho, you must already know everything, know it so well that you're already bored by the knowledge.

"Yes," I said, wearily, "it certainly does."

"Right off," he marveled.

"To the street," I concluded.

Well, that very night, that night of the Heavenly Theories, Mr. Mendoza came into the bar. The men stopped all their arguing and immediately taunted him: "Oh look! Saint Mendoza is here!" "Hey, Mendoza! Seen any angels lately?" He only smirked. Then, squaring his slender shoulders, he walked, erect, to the bar.

"Boy," he said to me. "A beer."

As I handed him the bottle, I wanted to confess: *I will change my ways! I will never peep at girls again!*

He turned and faced the crowd and gulped down his beer, emptying the entire bottle without coming up for air. When the last of the foam ran from its mouth, he slammed the bottle on the counter and said, "Ah!" Then he belched. Loudly. This greatly offended the gathered men, and they admonished him. But he ignored them, crying out, "What do you think of that! Eh? The belch is the

149

cry of the water buffalo, the hog. I give it to you because it is the only philosophy you can understand!"

More offended still, the crowd began to mumble.

Mr. Mendoza turned to me and said, "I see there are many wiggly feet present."

"The man's insane," said Crispin.

Mr. Mendoza continued: "Social change and the nipping at complacent buttocks was my calling on earth. Who among you can deny that I and my brush are a perfect marriage? Who among you can hope to do more with a brush than I?"

He pulled the brush from under his coat. Several men shied away.

"I tell you now," he said. "Here is the key to Heaven."

He nodded to me once, and strode toward the door. Just before he passed into the night he said, "My work is finished."

Tuesday morning we were up at dawn. Jaime had discovered a chink in fat Antonia's new roof. Through it, we could look down into her bedroom. We watched her dress. She moved in billows, like a meaty raincloud. "In a way," I whispered, "it has its charm."

"A bountiful harvest," Jaime said condescendingly.

After this ritual, we climbed down to the street. We heard the voices, saw people heading for the town square. Suddenly, we remembered. "Today!" we cried in unison.

The ever-growing throng was following Mr. Mendoza. His startling shock of white hair was bright against his dark skin. He wore a dusty black suit, his funeral suit. He walked into a corner of the square, knelt down, and pried the lid off a fresh can of paint. He produced the paint-brush with a flourish and held it up for all to see. There was an appreciative mumble from the crowd, a smatter-ing of applause. He turned to the can, dipped the brush in the paint. There was a hush. Mr. Mendoza painted a black swirl on the flagstones. He went around and around with the legendary brush, filling in the swirl until it was a solid black O. Then with a grin, with a virtuoso's mastery, he jerked his brush straight up, leaving a solid, glistening pole of wet paint standing in the air. We gasped. We clapped. Mr. Mendoza painted a horizontal line, connected to the first at a ninety-degree angle. We cheered. We whistled. He painted up, across, up, across, until he was reaching over his head. It was obvious soon enough. We applauded again, this time with feeling. Mr. Mendoza turned to look at us and waved once—whether in farewell or terse dis-missal we'll never know—then raised one foot and placed it on the first horizontal. *No,* we said. He stepped up. Fat Antonia fainted. The boys all tried to look up her dress when she fell, but Jaime and I were very macho because we'd seen it already. Still, Mr. Mendoza rose. He painted his way up, the angle of the stairway carrying him out of the plazuela and across town, over Bonifacio's crumbling church, over the cemetery where he had never slept and would apparently never sleep. Crispin did good business selling beers to the crowd. Mr. Mendoza, now small as a high-flying crow, climbed higher, over the Baluarte and its deadly bridge, over El Yauco and Kennedy's inverted nose, almost out of sight. The stairway wavered like smoke in the breeze. People were getting bored, and they began to wander off, back to work, back to the rumors. That evening, Jamie and I went back to fat Antonia's roof.

It happened on June fifth of that year. That night, at midnight, the rains came. By morning, the paint had washed away.

Eight

The White Girl

2 Short was a tagger from down around 24th Street. He hung with the Locos de Veinte set, though he freelanced as much as he banged. His tag was a cloudy blue-silver goth *II-SHT*, and it went out on freight trains and trucks all over the fucking place. His tag was, like, sailing through Nebraska and some shit like that. Out there, famous, large.

2 Short lived with his pops in that rundown house on W. 20th. That one with the black iron spears for a fence. The old-timer feeds shorties sometimes when they don't have anywhere to go—kids like Li'l Wino and Jetson. 2 Short's pops is a veterano. Been in jail a few times, been on the street, knows what it's like. He wants 2 Short to stay in school, but hey, what you gonna do? The vatos do what they got to do.

2 Short sometimes hangs in the backyard. He's not some nature pussy or nothing, but he likes the yard. Likes the old orange tree. The nopal cactus his pops cuts up and fries with eggs. 2 Short studies shit like birds and butterflies,

tries to get their shapes and their colors in his tag book. Hummingbirds.

Out behind their yard is that little scrapyard on 23rd. That one that takes up a block one way and about two blocks the other. Old, too. Cars in there been rusting out since '68. Gutierrez, the old dude runs the place, he's been scrapping the same hulks forever. Chasing kids out of there with a BB gun. *Ping!* Right in the ass!

2 Short always had too much imagination. He was scared to death of Gutiérrez's little kingdom behind the fence. All's you could see was the big tractor G used to drag wrecks around. The black oily crane stuck up like the stinger of the monsters in the sci-fi movies on channel 10. The Black Scorpion and shit.

The fence was ten feet tall, slats. Had some discolored rubber stuff woven in, like pieces of lawn furniture or something. 2 Short could only see little bits of the scary wrecks in there if he pressed his eye to the fence and squinted.

One day he just ran into the fence with his bike and one of those rotten old slats fell out and there it was — a passageway into the yard. He looked around, made sure Pops wasn't watching, listened to make sure G wasn't over there, and he slipped through.

Damn. There were wrecked cars piled on top of each other. It was eerie. Crumpled metal. Torn-off doors. Busted glass. He could see stars in the windshields where the heads had hit. Oh man—peeps died in here, homes.

2 Short crept into musty dead cars and twisted the steering wheels.

He came to a crunched '71 Charger. The seats were twisted and the dash was ripped out. Was that blood? On the old seat? Oh man. He ran his hand over the faded stain. *Blood.*

He found her bracelet under the seat. Her wrist must have been slender. It was a little gold chain with a little blue stone heart. He held it in his palm. Chick must have croaked right here.

He stared at the starred windshield. The way it was pushed out around the terrible cracks. Still brown. More blood. And then the hair.

Oh shit—there was hair in strands still stuck to the brown stains and the glass. Long blond strands of hair. They moved in the breeze. He touched them. He pulled them free. He wrapped them around his finger.

That night, he rubbed the hairs over his lips. He couldn't sleep. He kept thinking of the white girl. She was dead. How was that possible? How could she be dead?

He held the bracelet against his face. He lay with the hair against his cheek.

When he went out to tag two nights later, 2 Short aborted his own name. Die Hard and Arab said, "Yo, what's wrong with you?"

But he only said, "The white girl."

"What white girl, yo?"

But he stayed silent. He uncapped the blue. He stood

in front of the train car. *THE WHITE GIRL.* He wrote. It went out to New York. He sent it out to Mexico, to Japan on a container ship. *THE WHITE GIRL.*

He wrote it and wrote it. He sent it out to the world. He prayed with his can. He could not stop.

THE WHITE GIRL.
THE WHITE GIRL.
THE WHITE GIRL.

Nine

Young Man Blues

It sounded like a vacation spot: Pelican Bay.

But it was the opposite of that, and Joey's dad was going to be spending the next thirty-five years there in a cage. He'd left all his shit behind, and Joey spent his free time in the garage, sorting it out. Free time—what a laugh. Most of his time was free. That was part of the problem, though Joey knew his real job was keeping Moms afloat. When his dad went down, Moms got a tattoo right on her collarbone: WYATT. She cried alone when she thought Joey wasn't listening. Crying and the clinking of ice in her highball glass—Joey's lullaby.

Wyatt's stuff, the detritus of a lifetime, musty cardboard and paper feeding silverfish in the garage. Records and a turntable. Who had record players anymore? But the old man had loved his Technics turntable and his Infinity speakers that were almost as tall as Joey. And his cassette deck with wack faders so you could make suave mixtapes where the tunes seemed to swell out of each other. Joey had the stereo stacked at the foot of his bed, and he dragged in

161

records from the garage, where the old man kept them with his 1936 Indian Chief motorcycle. It leaned on its kickstand beneath the swastika flag—red and black and white and chrome under a couple of LED spotlights. The Indianhead light on the front fender was startling orange.

Joey hated taking the bus everywhere, but he was still too scared to try the big bike. Pops used to tell him it was alive, the knucklehead motor super-tuned and possessed by a speed devil. He'd ridden on it tucked in behind the old man—the bitch seat, Pops called it, though it was Moms who rode there, and he'd take down any fool who called her that. The old man's club colors would flap around in the wind and slap Joey in the face until he cried—the wind sucking his breath out from between his teeth, the whole world seeming to tip when Pops leaned into a curve, the roar moving up his ass into his gut and jetting up his spine till he thought he might lose the top of his head. It was a monster. Besides, it had a stick shift. Who'd ever seen a motorcycle with a stick shift?

All these records nobody'd ever heard of. But Pops said this was real music. This was real soul right here, real class, and anybody worth a damn would spin these disks and see the light. The black light, ha, am I right, Jo-Jo? Right, Dad. Study this shit like literature: Mose Allison, Blue Cheer, Three Man Army, SRC, Doug Kershaw, Bo Diddley.

I'm just twenty-two and I don't mind dyin'.

Muddy Waters, Electric Prunes, Aorta, Spirit, Crowbar.

"Living in the past, son. I'm just living in the past."

"I hear ya, Pops," Joey'd say.

He knew that was just an old Jethro Tull song.

Among the daggers and guns was some inexplicable stuff. Joey thought all of it was way-cool: cow skulls, a jackalope, a Mr. Bill bendable action figure, an eighteen-inch Alien figurine, a talking Pinhead doll from *Hellraiser*. He left the guns but put the toys in his room with the stereo.

Joey got up as usual at 6:30 and put on the coffeepot for his mom. She was dogged out every night from serving cocktails at the Catamaran. She had to step lively—the girls coming in behind her were young and hard and she was showing the miles, as she often said. She was still hot, his friends told him, which pretty much made him gag.

He heated up the coffee and cooked up a pan of oatmeal. He watched her sleeping on the couch, the TV turned on—her plasma night-light. Joey snuck her pack of Newports off the table and took them out to the trash can in back and covered them with the newspaper. The morning was all yellow and blue—sea air snapped in cold and salty. A lone gull looking tragic hung above him as if on a wire. Doves screwed in the palm trees with ridiculous rattling. A mockingbird dive-bombed Hobbes the tomcat. Back inside, Joey emptied the ashtray and poured out her hooch bottle before waking her.

He had work today. He was starting to like the job. It

was at Mrs. Filgate's house. The lady who used to work with Grandma at the Broadway. Nice lady—sold china. Little cups with pictures of German villages and shit on them.

On Mondays she had late shift, so she had to stay at the store until 9:00. This was no big deal, except she was married to this ancient dude—Freddie Filgate. Like, fifty years older than her or something. So Joey went to the Filgate house on the edge of Tecolote Canyon and worked on the yard all day. Then he sat with Mr. Filgate at night, made him his hot dogs and beans and watched the news and stuff until Mrs. Filgate came home and paid him $30. He'd take his money and walk a mile or so to the Dunkin' Donuts shop and visit with Sherri, the donut gal. Sooner or later he'd call one of his buds or Moms and they would drive by and pick him up.

Here's the great thing he loved about Freddie Filgate: he was so old he couldn't remember anyone's name, so he called everyone Willie. That cracked Joey up so bad: Willie. Reminded him of that record Pops had: *Willy and the Poor Boys*. It was hilarious. He liked being somebody else for a day.

⌘

Big Brother and the Holding Company, Quicksilver Messenger Service, Nazareth, Sabbath.

He was gentle with his mother. He took her big toe in his fingers and shook her leg. Purple nail polish, toe

164

rings, ankle bracelet. Freakin' Moms thought she was still a cheerleader at Clairemont High. She had a butterfly tattooed on her ankle, too. In memory of the baby she'd miscarried after Joey was born. His phantom sister.

"In-A-Gadda-Da-Vida, baby," he sang. "Dontcha know I love you?"

She stretched, yawned, opened her eyes. Put her hand over her mouth. Her eyes darted to the table, but her ciggies were gone. Bottle, too. Fleeting guilty smile.

"Jo-Jo," she said. "That was your dad's favorite song."

Joey nodded. He knew all about the old man's favorite songs. There were only about 1,347 of them.

"Got your gruel on the stove," he said. "Butter and syrup, right?"

"Yes, please."

"Raisins?"

"Yum."

She propped herself up with pillows—there was a red crease down her cheek like a scar. Her makeup was smeared. Moms had smearing eyes.

She turned up Matt Lauer with the remote as Joey brought her the steaming bowl and her coffee.

"You're a good boy."

"I know it."

"Got work today?"

"Yup."

"You be polite to Mr. Filgate."

"I will."

"They're good people."

Unlike us, he knew, was the hidden message in that particular comment. Well, he was cutting that happy crappy off at the pass. He thought they were all right. Not perfect, but fuck it.

"For sure," he said.

He put on his army coat. He'd painted the RAF bull's-eye on the back like The Who. He shoved his old man's Walkman deep in the pocket. Mixtapes in his other pocket. At least it had earbuds. People would think it was an iPod. He wiggled his mom's celly at her. She nodded. He slipped it in his back pocket. "Don't booty-dial me this time," she said.

He gave Moms a quick smooch and headed for the door.

"Honey?" she called.

"Yeah?"

"Got money?"

"Don't worry. I'm good," he said. He had seven dollars in his pocket. There was no work around here anywhere. If the old man hadn't taken the fall, Joey'd still be in Arizona, working for his uncle Victor putting in swamp coolers on Indian roofs in Sells. He'd been out there sleeping on Vic's couch since he'd dropped out. He glanced back at Moms. She was smiling at him with that *You're a dumbshit* look on her face. "Oh," he said. "You meant money for you."

He gave her the five and kept two bucks for bus fare and a donut.

"Love you," she said.

"Love you back."

It was the rule.

⌁

Pops had been Sergeant-at-Arms for the Visigoths MC. That was one reason Joey'd gone to Arizona. The war between the clubs.

Joey had Wyatt's colors in the closet on a hanger— the *VISIGOTHS* upper rocker curving down over a lurid iron fist, and the bottom patch curving back up, saying *DAGO*. *1%* on the front along with swastikas and the number *13* and a pentagram and some various German medals. They called him The Philosopher, since his name was Phil, Philip Wyatt, but mostly because of the crazy books he read. They were out in the garage with the big Indian and the Iron Butterfly records. The Philosopher or, yeah, more commonly, Philthy Phil. Joey smiled. He knew that if he stepped outside wearing the vest, he'd be dead in an hour. It gave the colors a weird sense of dark power. That kind of freaky-deaky stuff Pops was always reading about.

Joey shuffled along under the weak beach sun burning through the haze. He bobbed his head, rocking that Walkman, trying to understand Doug Kershaw's Cajun English, trying to see what Philthy Phil enjoyed about this fiddling country jam. His Chuck Taylors slapped on the sidewalk— half mile to the bus stop, catch the 8:00 up Balboa, transfer to the 8:38 number 5 down toward Tecolote Canyon, hop off at the old elementary school, and hoof it a half mile over to the Filgates'.

There's never been a man alive who lived his life and died fully satisfied.

He glanced around. He was paranoid. He thought he might make it to work as long as that fucking Butchie didn't come banging after him in his black 1968 Charger: Big Black. Butchie and his Mexicali gangster partner, Salvador. Out for blood.

❦

He made it to the corner in time to catch the bus. No freaks. No Big Black.

Joey sat in the backseat and listened to Jack Bruce sing about having a ticket to the waterfall. He loved that. Weird lyrics. Dreamy, like. Mysterious. He almost didn't notice the Charger pulling up behind the bus and cruising in its wake like a black barracuda.

Butchie and Salvador. It was all stupid, really. So lowlife, when you thought about it for a minute. Joey was pretty sure they'd leave Moms out of the ugly. She didn't have anything to do with it, aside from Butchie popping a boner every time he saw her. But he himself was starting to feel like he was toast.

The troubles had started when the Visigoths ran afoul of the Mongols. The Mongols did not approve of the new club forming and crowding the territory they'd already fought the Hells Angels over. When the war broke out, the Visigoths were doomed—you didn't take on the Mongols MC unless you were ready for Armageddon. Philthy Phil might have been ready, but guys like Butchie were not. Joey didn't know if Pops did the shooting, but somebody did. And when Pops was taken in, he'd left hidden weapons in the garage. Including Butchie's WWII Nazi Luger.

The club disbanded, and the smart members moved to Nevada. But Butchie wanted his gun back. When he came sniffing around, Joey had stupidly lied to him. He didn't even know why—after all, he had all his dad's crap. Butchie didn't know he was lying, though he figured everybody was a crook. He was studying Wyatt's boy like a textbook, looking for the penetration points. He could swallow the Luger scam if this new play paid off. Though Joey would still probably have to pay, get a li'l discipline for lying to Uncle Butchie.

Butchie'd shown up at the screen door while Moms was at work last night. He was raggedy and yellow-eyed. Two big Rottweilers in tow.

"Jo-Jo," he said. "You seen a fine example of German military design hereabouts?" He sniffed and giggled.

"What's that?" Joey said, looking at the beasts standing behind Butchie.

"Aryan dog flesh, Jo-Jo. That's what that is. Diesel and Death."

169

The big dogs slobbered and grinned when Butchie said their names.

"I don't know nothin' about no gun," Joey said.

"Who said anything about a gun?" Butchie cried. He'd been sniffing some joy, for sure. He waggled an accusatory finger at Joey.

"Yo," said Joey, thinking fast, "what else would it be? Like, a Panzer tank?" He snorted.

Butchie scratched his chin: whiskers went *scritch*.

"Cool," he said. "But see you tomorrow? We cool? You cool with that?"

"I guess," Joey replied.

"Cool!" Butchie enthused. "Come on, children." He shook the chains and the dogs shuffled after him.

❧

Joey was stuck. Butchie had been hanging out at the Catamaran, dropping sweet tips and sweet talk on Moms, all to get a handle on the whole Filgate scenario.

The Philosopher had drunkenly spoken of the old man's antiques and samurai swords and big glass water jug full of change (probably $300 right there) in that house. That locked-up house—had locks on the gate and locks on the garage and about five deadbolts inside, and Butchie and Salvador were going to wait till Joey was inside to unlock Fort Knox for them. Hell, they'd already dreamed up gun collections and aged bourbon in hundred-dollar bottles.

All Joey had to do was open the door. Butchie figured Jo-Jo owed him that much.

Butchie lounged around like a dirty shirt hung on a nail, his teeth black at the roots, his tweaked-out eyeballs jumping like Mexican souvenir beans in little bone bowls. He had a waxed-up flattop haircut like some bogus marine.

Pops had dissed Butchie round the clock. Loser. Joey was thinking about this when he got off the bus and hustled to the stop in front of Del Taco. Screw it—he was early. He was going on down to Dunkin' to see if Sherri was in. Sometimes, though she worked late nights, she hung out in the shop with a tall coffee and some day-olds and shot the shit with the day girls. Ever since her divorce, she had no place else to go.

But what he really liked was that she was the only chick he'd ever met who had read the same books as Philthy Phil. Crazy books—she actually had the same paperback *Necronomicon Spellbook* that Pops had. And it was cool that she was older. She could tell him all about the secret magic signals in Zeppelin songs. There was nobody around now with secret stuff in songs like that. Well, maybe Tool. But he didn't understand what Tool were talking about.

Sometimes he'd sit there with her until the morning shift showed up, and he couldn't tell how he'd stayed all night.

He was hurrying down the sidewalk when he felt the blackness sidle up to him. *Damn*. He pulled out the earbuds, and there it was: that Hemi engine gurgling through those twin glasspack pipes. That hot rod sound Moms called "rocks in a coffee can." The long front fender of the Charger slid along beside him. Diesel and Death in the backseat like fat grandmothers.

Salvador rolled down his window.

"Jo-Jooooo," he taunted. Yo-Yooooo.

"Hey, hotshot," Butchie shouted from the driver's seat. "We got a date tonight! Don't screw it up. Hear me?"

Joey looked at them.

"It's your dad's play, Jo-Jo," Butchie called. "I didn't think it up. And. Uh. You, like, owe it to us."

"Yeah," said Salvador.

He was pointing his finger at Joey.

"Pow pow pow," he said.

Joey didn't even get what about that was making them laugh.

"Whoa!" shouted Butchie. He held up a fist. "Knock it!" He and Salvador bumped knuckles.

"Blow it up!" Their hands flew apart, mouths went *BWOOSH!* "Make it rain!" Their fingers wiggled past their faces. "Hey!" Butchie hollered. "You goin' down to buy a donut?"

Joey shook his head right away.

"No? You look like a man looking for a donut!"

"How 'bout a churro?" Salvador asked.

This utterly busted up Butchie and he swerved and smacked the wheel.

"Beaner's the tits, ain't he, Jo-Jo?" he shrieked.

Joey nodded.

"You're sweet on that Sylvester Stallone–lookin' bitch in the donut shop. Am I right?"

Joey shook his head.

Salvador smacked his hand on the side of the Charger.

"I know all. Yeah?" Butchie called. "There are no secrets. So! Tonight, right? To-night!"

Joey shrugged.

"Yes?"

"Okay, okay. Yeah," Joey said. His face was burning. He was not ashamed. But he was blushing like a mofo, and he felt dizzy. He felt like a tornado was coming down the street and his feet were caught in a huge wad of bubble gum.

"My man!"

"We be outside, güey!" Salvador shouted. "Waiting."

"Just open that goddamned door," Butchie said and shifted hard and chirped the tires as he burned away from the curb in massive blue exhalations and fartings as Big Black forced a Prius out of its way.

Joey turned back, worrying about Freddie Filgate. He didn't have the heart to see Sherri now. He put in the buds. *A young man don't mean nothin' in the world today.*

✍

The yard went down the slope of the canyon in seven terraces. Freddie had lime trees, orange trees, and lemon trees down there. One ill banana. The slopes below were crowded with ice plant. Freddie called it "pickle weed" and said it stopped wildfires.

At the top, Mrs. Filgate had her roses. Joey didn't know a thing about roses. All she told him was to trim the branches. He was trying to snip away with the little shears, and the thorns were doing a number on his fingers. Freddie ambled out of the house with a glass of lemonade.

"Willie," he said. "You need to hydrate."

"Thank you, Freddie."

"Cut those twigs at an angle, son. Not straight across. Roses are oblique in personality, Willie. They like things angled."

Joey smiled. Freddie was a trip.

He snipped.

"Like that?"

"Now you're cooking, Willie. Cooking with gasoline."

Freddie smacked his big hands together. They sounded soft and dusty. White as paper. Freddie's little straw hat had a green plastic insert in its brim and cast colored light down on half his face. His glasses were about nine inches thick. He had hearing aids in his ears. One of them whistled and squealed. He shuffled around in slippers, his big old man pants tucked up to his ribs.

"God is great," Freddie Filgate said.

"Can I ask you something?" said Joey, carefully snipping the rose branches. He didn't have any gloves. He was thinking: *OW*, and *FUCK*, and *BITCH* as the thorns poked his fingers. But he would never say those words in front of Freddie.

"Ask away, ask away," said Freddie, waving a hand as he stared out at the canyon.

"Ah, hmm," muttered Joey. "I was wondering how old you are. If that ain't rude."

He gulped his lemonade.

"Rude! Oh my! Saying 'ain't' in educated company is what's rude, Willie!" Freddie chuckled in his whispery way. "I am ninety-two and a half. But who's counting? Heard an owl last night, Willie. Apache Indians consider that a sign of death. But I'm not ready for that yet. Not by a long shot!"

"And Mrs.?"

"She is in the springtime of her life. A blushing and dewy sixty-one."

Freddie smiled at Joey, and Joey smiled at Freddie.

He took Joey's glass and walked back toward the house.

"Bologna on onion buns. Mustard. Sound good? Finish up and join me," he called. "It's almost dinnertime."

Joey snipped branches and worried about Butchie and sucked tiny beads of blood off his fingers.

Freddie kept it burning hot inside. Joey figured it was an old guy thing—that and the musty smell. It smelled like mildew and Mentholatum and potpourri. He slipped out to the kitchen and peeked out the front window. No Big Black yet. *What if the old dude don't tell you where the good stuff is, Butchie? Shit, Jo-Jo, old men break real easy.*

Freddie cut the onion buns in quarters and put potato chips beside each sandwich. He did everything neatly. The whole house was squared away. "Mrs. Filgate says I would use a spirit level to make sure the Christmas tree is straight every year, but she won't let me," Freddie had told him.

Joey sat down. The plates were plastic. The sandwiches were thin. That had to be another old guy thing—not eating much.

"Let us give thanks, Willie."

Joey put his elbows on the table and folded his hands in front of his face. He didn't know anything about prayers, but he liked that Freddie did.

"Sweet Lord," Freddie said. "We come together in fellowship and gratitude. Thank you for this day, for this food, and for this life. May we make the most of them. In Your holy name we pray. Amen."

"Um," Joey said. He was listening for that big engine outside.

"Through the teeth and over the gums, look out belly, here it comes," said Freddie.

Joey laughed. Every time he heard a car, he stopped chewing. "Good one, Freddie," he said.

Dusk was turning the upper edges of the windows slightly maroon.

Freddie said, "Are you a man of faith, Willie?"

"Faith?"

"Are you a praying man?"

Joey was already done with his sandwich. He scarfed up the rest of his chips and reached for the bag. "Not," he said, "really."

"Because I notice you didn't say grace."

Joey got up and looked out the window. He got a pitcher down from the cabinet and filled it with water. Got a red Kool-Aid and some sugar and stirred it in. The Filgates had plastic glasses with Mexican colors painted around the rims.

"Ice, Freddie?" he said.

"Oh, no. Ice is a little too strong for me."

Joey brought the glasses to the table, collected the plastic plates, and took them to the sink. Quick glance. SHIT! There was Big Black, pulled over to the curb across the street. He could see the two idiots in the front seat, masses of shadow like big piles of spoiling meat.

Freddie had bits of chip stuck to his lips. He slurped his red drink. Joey handed him a napkin. His hands were shaking.

"I didn't get no church or nothin'," he said. "Didn't really, you know, learn to pray. Much."

"Ah, Willie," Freddie sighed.

Butchie couldn't get in if Joey just ignored him. The doors were locked tight. But he imagined the Visigoths putting their big boots to the wood until it broke. Then what?

"You see, son," Freddie was saying. "You don't need a church to pray. Why, we are the church. Yes sir. You and I. Right here! Isn't that wonderful?"

Joey was staring at Freddie, his mind racing.

"I never studied up on that," he said.

He went to wash the plates and the glasses and keep an eye on Big Black. It was almost dark. Butchie had turned on the inner light, and Joey could see him tossing snacks over the seat to his hounds. Suddenly, Butchie turned his head and stared back at Joey. Backlit, his face was buried in shadow.

Freddie appeared with a carved wooden dove. "Look here," he said. "I whittled it myself. How about you take that to your momma?"

WTF, Freddie. Seriously.

"Holy Spirit," Freddie said, as if imparting some great secret.

Big Black's door opened. Butchie got out, walked around, shook his leg. Stood with his hands on his hips, staring. He pointed at Joey. Got back in and slammed the car door.

"Willie, come," said Freddie. Joey went back to the table where Freddie was sitting. He pulled his mom's cell phone out of his pocket and set it down beside the dove. Freddie said, "I pray, son. Every day. And now that my time is short, God has rewarded me with visions."

"Visions, Freddie?"

"I was shown the meaning of life, Willie. I was on my

knees in that very corner, and the walls peeled back and angels were before me."

"Right here on Cowley Way?" said Joey.

Screw Butchie—that dick.

"The street was gone, Willie. What was before me? Nothing but light."

Freddie patted the table as if it were his favorite pet— as if the table could feel his touch.

"And God showed me. This table is not made of wood. This table is made of light."

Joey fingered the celly. Mrs. Filgate would be home in an hour. And then?

"Atoms, electrons. Yes?" Joey nodded while Freddie continued. "At base, pure energy. Pure...light. And we are made of it. Everything is made of them. Let there be light. And there was light. Every one of us, even the least of us, is a creature of mere light, Willie. Light. Oh, amen. Can you say 'amen'?"

"Amen," said Joey.

He went to the bathroom and flipped open the phone and linked to the police station and said, "There's some, like, crooks casing houses on Cowley Way. I think they're going to rip off this old man named Freddie Filgate. We're really worried." He gave the address. "They're sitting outside in a black Charger. Hurry."

He turned off the light in the kitchen and watched out the window. Freddie had already retired to the blue glow of *American Pickers* on cable. The police cruiser came down the street, creeping. They hit Butchie with a spotlight. Oh yes—panic inside Big Black. Butchie fired up the engine and pulled out and glared at the house. Joey stuck his hand in the window and shot him the finger as Big Black moved out with the white cop car tagging behind.

Joey was dead meat now. Freddie had started to snore. His bad hearing aid wailed in his ear. Joey took a crocheted caftan and put it over the old man's legs and sat there wondering how you started a prayer without sounding like an asshole.

*

Mrs. Filgate had given him his $30 and a $10 bonus for doing such a good job on her roses. Joey was jogging in the dark, pausing at every corner to make sure Butchie and Salvador weren't waiting to set the hounds on him. He was going to see Sherri, man, especially tonight. He just knew if he was near Sherri something good was going to happen. He'd be all right with her. It was coming on him in one big rush: Sherri, Sherri, Sherri.

He knew he could cut through the Buena Vista apartment complex and be safe for most of five blocks, cutting in and out of the buildings, scrambling across alleys like a cat. He was home free. Those losers were gone. He put in his buds.

Shawn Phillips. Tom Rush. Chet Baker. Biff Rose.

He watched the traffic on the main drag, not happy about all the lights. But there was no Big Black in sight either way, not hiding behind the bowling alley, not down the hill in the big parking lot of Vons market. Clear. He ran across, slapping his high-tops loud and sharp and the bell over the door in the donut shop pinged and Sherri came out from the back room and smiled at him.

"Hi."

"Hi."

"How you?"

"Good. You?"

"Slow, hon. Slow night."

He stared at her.

She busied herself with rearranging the bear claws. She glanced up at him, leaning on the glass case. She had this way of looking up from under her brows. She said, "What?"

"Nothin'."

She gave him that woman-smile and said, "You don't look like it's nothing."

"Sherri," he said. "Do you pray?"

"I prayed you'd come in tonight," she said.

She laughed when his mouth opened and nothing came out.

"Cutie," she said.

Light. Everything is made of light. Me. Sherri. Light.

"Can I touch your cheek?" he blurted. He was in uncharted territory now. He was flying into a cloud.

Real slow, she leaned forward. She moved her hair away from her face. She closed her eyes. He swallowed. He reached across the counter and laid his hand on her cheek.

181

She had three piercings in her ear. Her skin was so soft. He rubbed it with his thumb. She opened her eyes. He took his hand away.

Hazel eyes.

"What was that, Joey?" she asked.

"I…" Light. "I don't know."

They laughed a little. Faces red. She breathed deep and shook her head and knitted her brow a little and stared.

A car pulled up. Cut its lights. He went to a table in the far end of the shop and listened to her sell a sailor a dozen donut holes. When she'd rung him up and he'd banged back out, she unlocked the white door to the back room and peeked out.

"You want to come keep me company while I cook donuts?" she said.

"Can I?"

She shrugged one shoulder.

"Who'll know?"

She was grinning real wicked now. And he was feeling his pulse inside his jeans. From a touch? It was her look. Her smile. It was the smile. He was feeling fire and fluid deep down inside himself.

He got up. He shambled toward her. Light. Light. Light. He went in the back room. She closed the door and locked it. Bags everywhere of flour. Bags of sugar. Plastic jugs full of chocolate. It smelled like sugar and grease. Sherri smelled like sugar. His jaws hurt. His heart raced. She stood too close to him.

Her body was hot in her white donut shop uniform. He could feel her. He stared at her face. He stared at her breasts. She had powdered sugar on her hands. His hands were shaking again. She breathed into his face.

"Joey," she said, softly.

He closed his eyes.

"Do you want to touch my breasts?"

"Yes."

"You can."

"Okay."

He looked, and she had turned toward him. He put his hand out—only one finger at first. He touched her breast where he thought her nipple was. Her bra was dense and thick. He pressed softly, but didn't feel anything but layers of cotton.

"Don't be afraid," she said.

He cupped her breast and held her. He put his other hand on her other breast. She moved the zipper of her frock down. He put his face to her cleavage. He smelled her. He breathed her all in. All the sugar and her sweat and her perfume and he could smell her lotion and her shampoo and her laundry soap and he pressed his mouth to her and said, "Could you call me Willie?" And she sighed and pulled the material aside. He took her nipple in his mouth.

"Willie," she said.

He had just begun to weep when the bell dinged and Butchie came into the shop.

Ten

Chametla

The last shot fired in the Battle of Chametla hit Private Arnulfo Guerrero in the back of the head. It took out the lower-right quadrant, knocking free a hunk of bone roughly the size and shape of a broken teacup. This shot was fired by a federal trooper, who then shouldered his weapon and walked to a cantina on the outskirts of town, where he ate a fine pork stew with seven corn tortillas and a cup of pulque. The shot was witnessed by Guerrero's best friend, Corporal Ángel García, and by Guerrero's dog, Casan. Casan was a floppy-eared Alsatian he'd stolen from a federales base the year before.

"Por Dios, Arnulfo," García muttered as he stuffed straw and a long strip of his tunic into the gaping head wound. "What have they done to you?"

Guerrero writhed on the ground, his teeth clenched in a silent rage, froth collecting on his lips.

García stanched the bleeding and wrapped a dirty field dressing around and around his friend's head.

Casan stood to the side, whining and fretting.

187

Troops were everywhere, and though the Battle of Chametla was over, García didn't know it. So he pulled his comrade onto his shoulders in a straining carry—for Guerrero was at least a foot taller and many pounds heavier—and struggled to a copse of cottonwoods beside a muddy creek. He put his friend down gently on a bed of leaves and cottonwood fluff, and he tied Casan's rope leash to the trunk. Then he snuck down to the creek and filled his hat with water. He tried to wet his friend's lips, but the dying man was already too far gone to drink.

They'd come out of the mining lands of Rosario, Sinaloa, full of revolution and fun. Men were raised to fight and enjoy fighting. None dared admit they were weary of it, weary of fear, and each had learned to dream, and dreamed at all hours—dreamed while sleeping, while awake and marching, while fighting. Only dreaming carried them through the unending battles.

They'd drunk their fill, slept with country girls in every village, ridden trains to battle. Both Guerrero and García were excited by the trains—their first train rides. Then they were sickened by the rocking of the freight cars and choked by the smoke boiling back over the roof, where they fought for space and tried not to be forced off. They coughed black cinders at night.

Casan was just one of their treasures, one of the fruits of their exploits. They'd stolen guitars, rifles, horses. Guerrero had stolen underwear from haciendas, and García himself had stolen a cigar from the pocket of a sleeping federal captain. They'd seen men hang and watched villages burn.

"Don't die now, you bastard," García grunted as he peeked out through the bushes to see if their enemies had fled. "We have so much to do!"

But Guerrero only moaned and kicked his feet.

As night fell, Ángel García gathered wood. He peeled back the sullied bandages to let air and moonlight in. The ugly black cavern blown out of Guerrero's head leaked slow and watery blood. His face was pale. His skin was cold. And still he drew breath and occasionally stirred and mumbled.

García lit a small fire and moved Guerrero nearer to the flames. He tore long strips from his friend's shirt and rewrapped his head. Why waste a swallow of tequila on him? There was a bottle in his bedroll. He lifted it in a silent toast and drank.

He must have drifted off to sleep, for it was Casan's whimpering that awoke him. The big dog had worked himself free from the rope, and he stood over the prone body of Guerrero and whined.

"What is it, boy?" García whispered.

Casan tilted his head and stared down at Guerrero. The dog yelped. Then he backed away.

García crawled over to Guerrero and said, "Arnulfo? Are you awake?"

The wounded man didn't stir.

"What the hell is wrong with you?" García chided the dog. "Nothing here."

Then he heard it too. The faint whistling. He inclined his head. There was a plaintive hooting coming from under Guerrero's bandage. Were poor Guerrero's sinuses blowing air out of his skull? Christ. What next? García pulled open the wrapping and was startled to see a small puff of smoke rising from out of his friend's head. He crossed himself.

"Ah, cabrón!" he said.

The whistle again, then another puff of smoke. Casan barked. García sat beside the dog and stared. Then, was it? It couldn't be! But—a light—a small light was coming out of the ragged hole in Guerrero's head.

García bent down, but then had to leap back because a tiny locomotive rushed out of Guerrero's wound. It fell out of the wound, pulling a coal car and several small cattle cars as if it were falling off a minuscule bridge in some rail disaster. The soft train fell upon the ground and glistened, puffing like a fish. Casan pounced on it and took it in his mouth, shaking it once and gulping it down.

"Bad dog!" said García.

But by then, Guerrero's childhood home had squeezed out of his head. It was quite remarkable. The walls were soft and pink, and the furniture was veiny and tender. Casan ate the back porch. García, starving after the battle, skewered the couch, the bed, and the oven on a wire and roasted them over the fire. They tasted like pork.

Guerrero grunted once and a pile of schoolbooks plopped out.

Soon, García was appalled to see Guerrero's parents and

boyhood friends. Their cries were puny and heartrending when Casan ate them. And naked women! Good God! He didn't know Guerrero had mounted so many naked women! He looked carefully—they came out in a parade of breasts and asses, small legs waving. He couldn't bear it. He couldn't bear his own lust and his own hunger, and he couldn't bear Casan's insatiable mouth, and he couldn't bear his own loneliness. If he had tried to make love to them, he would have torn them apart.

All these small beings mewled and quickly expired.

It was the worst night of his life. He found himself praying that Guerrero would die. But he didn't die. And García decided, finally, irrevocably, that he had to leave his friend to his fate. The damage to his own soul would be too great if he sat there any longer watching children, priests, grandmothers, goats, wagons, and toys ooze out of Guerrero's bloody head and die on the ground. So he put the rope through Casan's collar, and he tucked Guerrero's pistol in his own belt, and he put Guerrero's boots on his own feet, and he made his friend as comfortable as possible.

Birds gathered. First, crows. Then magpies and robins. Finally, gulls came from the coast. They seemed to be praying to Guerrero, for they bowed to him repeatedly. They stayed there and fed on his dreams until they were too heavy to fly.

Eleven

The Sous Chefs of Iogüa

For Trinity Ray

Saturday. Lunch. Dexter Bower couldn't find his red baseball cap anywhere and had to make do with the tan cap with a fish stitched to the front. That irked the crap out of him, but maybe that's just what happens when you get old. Everything's so damned irksome. Like the Mexican farmhands. They couldn't say the name of the state if you paid them.

Dexter grunted. Of course, he *was* paying them. Those boys worked hard, worked as his momma used to say till their finger bones were poppin'. But they couldn't say "Iowa" in schoolyard English and it came out like this: "Eee-uh-güey."

Plenty of people, of course, still said "Ioway" and that didn't bother him at all. That was traditional. That was English, for Godsakes.

He liked how they called him "Jefe," though. He pronounced it "Heffy." He hadn't enjoyed school all that much, but they could have warned him that language would prove overtaxing.

"Iowa. See?"

He'd worked on it with a pencil stub and a sheet of notebook paper with his foreman, Juan. Juan was from someplace near Guadalajara. Tlaquepaque. How were you supposed to say that?

Juan smiled and shook his head and stared. Mexicans said lots of things with their smiles and head shakes. Mostly, Dex believed, they were saying, *Don't fire me, Jefe*.

He'd finally compromised on the phonetics. He wrote the word out like this: *IOGUA*. Felt like a United Nations ambassador.

That was when Juan still worked for him. Bunked out in the workers' shed. Now Juan had moved into town and opened a restaurant, and that's where Dexter was headed. To see if Juan had taken any steps to heal the various damages done to Ioway by all this upheaval and displacement.

"Ee-uh-guey," he muttered to himself, as he dragged himself into the F-150.

That lower back wasn't doing nobody any good. He chuffed out a laugh. Who was he kidding? Ol' Pedro, running the restaurant across the street from Juan's—why, hell, everybody called that poor guy "Pee-dro." It was all a new language around here now.

Like that clown on NPR said: *The paradigm has shifted. Every American town is a border town now.*

"Jesus."

♂♀

Dexter farmed 1,500 acres and leased another hundred-acre share to the east. Like everybody else, he had it divided between corn and soy. He ran a few handsome spotted cows on ten acres, selling off calves every year. And he was experimenting with sorghum and hay and things like that. Getting some nitrogen back into the soil.

So far he had managed to avoid using all that Monsanto demon seed—that bioengineered stuff that was half moray eel on the genetic level, or had spider blood in it instead of sap, or glowed with firefly juice in the kernels. Shit was what that was. Killing off all the goddamned bees. He could spit. He rolled down the window, took a breath, and went ahead and let fly.

"Bastards," he said.

He kept his truck clean and his house tidy. She had always kept it neat, and he saw no reason to sully her memory with clutter or fuss. The porches were swept and the rockers sat there, jaunty in the sun, as if expecting herself to reappear at any moment and sit there reading one of her book club books. But she was gone now more than two years.

She had planted them a nice vegetable and herb garden, and when Juan still worked for him, he'd tended to the edibles—Juan was a wizard, all right. Dexter didn't really care for kale or cabbage or cauliflower, which was too bad because Ol' Juan brought it in by the gunnysack. Tomatoes, iceberg lettuce, cukes, squash, pumpkins. It was nice. Nice herbs, too—though Juan had snuck in all this Mexican stuff and Dexter was half-convinced there was marijuana in there somewhere. Cilantro? No thanks—tasted like soap.

Dexter drove his half-mile track out to the state road. Every winter he'd be out here plowing with the big red blade mounted on the Ford, and when he was done opening up his drive, he'd by God get cracking on the neighbors' spreads down the road. Arnie and Ina, good Vikings from Minnesota. The Rays over to the east—they had a kid. Couldn't be trapped out here in snow. That's how America worked. Used to work. That was what made things function. It was all obvious come winter. Some folks wouldn't pitch in with a snow shovel if they saw a naked one-hundred-year-old lady out there struggling with a drift. Of course, there had been no winter to speak of this year. His damn crab apple tree was already blooming. Dex fretted about the day he could no longer steer the plow. Who would help the neighbors then?

Ina the Viking was out in her potato patch waving at him like some idiot. Some people thought life was just the spiffiest thing that ever happened. Dexter raised one finger off the top of the wheel in greeting and roared down the blacktop toward West Linden, sun flashing like emergency flares off all the corners of his rig.

⌘

Juan Reyes sat in his dark restaurant on 5th Street with his head resting on one hand. The bowl of menudo before him blew steam into his face. The cloud was scented with the delicious essence of tripe and lime juice and cilantro and Cholula sauce and diced red onions. Fat hominy lurked in the murky red soup like a hundred eyes watching him eat. He took a wide spoon and delivered a shot of lava to his mouth and slurped it like a great mule at a water trough. He loved the way the tripe fought his teeth. Oh, but he was hungover. La cruda. Ta' cabrona. His head crunched rhythmically in his skull. Everybody except gringos knew the only way to cure hangovers was with menudo and enough Cholula to make you weep blood.

Americans! What barbarians. He couldn't get an American to sit down to a bowl of menudo if he were paying them. They didn't like Mexican food unless it was smothered in sour cream and melted yellow cheese. They didn't care if the cheese was squirted from a can—as long as it was hot and yellow and copious. On their flour tortillas. Texas food, not Mexican food. Juan had never tasted sour cream until he was ten years old. He thought cheese was white and came from a goat. And he ate his first flour tortilla in Juárez.

Ah, menudo. His customers didn't know what they were missing. He sipped his cinnamon coffee. It wasn't just menudo—they didn't come in anymore for anything. He was certain the recent vogue in fish tacos would enliven his business, but the Iowans had lost their interest in Taquería Los Reyes. His brother Hugo had gone off to Chicago, where he could make fancy Asian fusion banana and green tea leaf enchiladas in West Pilsen for the hipster Yuppies and Chuppies there.

Occasionally, college kids from Iowa City came down to West Linden and stopped by. Nerdy glasses and earrings and hilarity. They had come for ironic meals. Mexican food in the midwestern heartland. Jajajajaja.

It was his old El Jefe, Señor Dexter, who pointed out the problem. He'd been the only client, again. Eating carnitas of pork in red sauce, again. Juan had sat with him and let slip that business was so far down that he might have to close the taquería and return to the farm.

"Do you think," he had asked his old boss, "is an anti-immigrant thing?"

Dexter Bower had glared at him with that hawkeye of his.

"You're asking me if they're racists?" he demanded.

Juan shrugged.

Dexter scooted his chair back and said, "C'mere."

They stepped out the door onto 5th Street.

"Main Street," Dexter said. "USA."

"Sí."

"Two trucks and a Cadillac."

Juan, nodding.

"This isn't New York City, Juan. This is West Linden."

"Yes."

"You boys came in here and picked our crops. Then you knew a good thing when you saw it and started to settle. The migrant workers left guys and gals here like seeds. Am I right?"

"You right, Jefe."

"And you made restaurants."

"We did. Good ones!"

"Not arguing that, Juan," Dexter said. "But we didn't have but three restaurants in town. Now look."

He pointed all around him.

Taquería Los Reyes. Across the street, Pedro's Así Es Mi Tierra. Down the block, Araceli's Cantina La Buena.

"There's nothin' but tacos on this goddamn street, Juan! Pee-dro over there was the last one to move in and that just about tore it. Man, how many tacos do you expect a fellow to eat? The mayor has been begging McDonald's to open a place here for a year just to eat a cheeseburger!"

"Caray," said Juan. "What do I do?"

Dexter Bower, the sun on the sidewalk, offered wisdom: "Diversify."

ふ

Dexter drove past the cemetery and turned his head away. He still couldn't bear to look in there. Didn't like catching himself counting the stones till he found hers. Didn't like feeling guilty that he hadn't left flowers lately. All flowers did was wilt and turn brown.

A thousand miles of bright land swam around the road.

He didn't know what the hell people were talking about when they called Iowa dull. The fields were the deepest green and brightest gold on earth. The sky blew high with piles of electric clouds. And grackles and crows flew between cottonwoods and fence posts. He loved it, loved it like a girlfriend. From the bluffs on the Mississippi to the flat acres of tilled crops. He loved the barns and the silos and the old trucks and the horses drooping under shade trees and the watering holes. Sunflowers.

He loved the road and the turtles sneaking across it from pond to pond and the boys riding their bikes down dirt lanes. And he loved West Linden—looked for the barbershop where his dad had had his hair cut and his son did too, looked at the green square with its old cannon, looked to see if the flag was at half-mast, looked to see if the bookstore was open. He was a little sweet on the widow McGinnis, but he was shy, didn't know how long was long enough before he could go courting. But he bought lots of used detective paperbacks from her. He even tried one of her mocha lattes from time to time. Dessert in a cup. She always tried to put whipped cream on it. He guffawed and rattled over frost heaves slathered with tar stripes. Dexter went so far as to like the ridiculous cell tower somebody had built to look like an incongruous giant pine tree. He liked it that a tornado had never hit them yet.

Well, the Mexicans had hit, that was true. But without them, he could not have afforded to keep farming. Now that most of them were gone—except for Juan and his busboys and wife—the Bower farm was in serious trouble. There were no kids around anymore to take up the slack, and even if there were, he couldn't get them to bend to a hoe if he paid them three times what he paid the Mex-ies. When he gave away free pumpkins in October, the lazy sons of bitches didn't even come out to pick their own. He had to pile them in the F-150 and give them away on the square.

"Hell in a handbasket," he muttered, as he parked in the diagonal slot in front of Juan's Italian Cuisine—We Cook American.

He stared at the window and shook his head.

It said: ESPECIAL TODAY—ESPAGETI!

Well, at least Juan was trying.

"What the hell is this?" Dexter said.

"Jefe! Is espageti!"

Dex looked at the generous pile of pasta and the thick red sauce. Mushrooms. That was good. Garlic bread (even though it was a Mexican bolillo). What baffled Dexter was the sliced hard-boiled eggs.

He pointed at the plate and glared at Juan.

"What?" said Juan.

It sounded like *Guah?*

"Eggs? In spaghetti?" Dexter demanded.

"Claro!"

"Who the hell eats eggs in spaghetti, is what I'm asking you."

Juan looked stricken.

"Nosotros. Is my father's recipe, pues."

He said *receipt*. The "p" was not silent.

"Juan! The idea was to make real American Eye-talian food. This is…this is …Mexican spaghetti."

Juan sat.

"This is very hard, Jefe."

Dexter tasted the food. It was weird. But, he had to admit, tasty. Eggs. 'Bout made him barf. He ate some more.

Beto the busboy was watching soccer on a small TV near the register. Carmela, Juan's vastly pregnant wife, sat sideways in a booth with her feet up, snoring softly. Across the room, Preacher Visser was digging into a plate. A good Presbyterian—he had done the funeral for the Bowers. His hat sat on the table.

"Rev," Dexter said.

Visser waved with one hand and kept eating.

"What are you having?" Dexter asked.

"Chicken parm, with a glass of Chianti. Delicious."

"Early for wine," Dex couldn't help noting.

"Good enough for Jesus," the reverend replied.

Juan grinned at Beto and said, "Mira este cabrón." They laughed.

Juan leaned across the table. "Jefe?" he whispered. "It's Hungry Man. Microwave." He raised his hands. "They don' know the difference."

Dex was rankled.

"Look here," Dexter said. "I told you—you want Americans in here, make pizzas. And not like that tostada you made last time. Not—" he hissed so the pastor wouldn't hear—"*television dinners!*"

Juan sighed.

"Pizzas," he said, as if someone had just suggested something deeply heretical to a priest. He called them *peeksas*. "I would have to get an oven."

Beto ambled over and refilled the pastor's glass.

"Peeksas," Juan continued. "I know, I know, Jefe. Peeksas and calzones."

"Meatball torpedo would be nice," the rev said.

"Submarine," Dexter corrected.

"Guah?" said Juan.

"In Boston," the rev announced, "we called them grinders."

"Qué?"

Dexter made a *what have I been sayin'* gesture.

"Pizzas. Calzones. Get the oven. Take orders by phone. Make Beto deliver."

"I ain't driving no delivery car," Beto said and went back to his game.

Calzones. He smirked. Gringos didn't know that meant underpants.

"If you won't do it, Juan can give that fine job to a deserving white man!"

"Now, Dex," the rev chided him.

Juan shook his head. "No like. You hurtin' me now."

Dexter had just about had it with this happy horseshit and was thinking about driving back to his house and cracking a beer and to hell with it. There was a *Deadliest Catch* marathon on the dish. Not a Mexican in sight!

"All right. I am sorry."

"Have beer," Juan said.

"Sí, sí." Dex rubbed his forehead. "¿Cómo no?"

⌖

The three of them stood out on the sidewalk. Juan, Dexter Bower, and Preacher Visser—who had a plastic glass of wine in his mitt. Across the street, Pedro's Velvet Dragon Chinese Restaurant seemed to be doing fair business. Better than Juan's Italian.

Dexter looked down at Araceli's Mom's Cantina. He had scolded her—"cantina" was not American in any way, and didn't go with "Mom's" no matter what language you were speaking. Christ on a waffle—these people were like children.

Pinches gringos, Juan was thinking. *Sangrones*.

Dex had told Araceli to call it Mom's Café, damn it! He had bellowed, "I am just trying to help!" and all the staff at Mom's had hidden in the kitchen and wondered why gringos shouted their heads off all the time. They thought that if you had an accent, you were deaf. If they just screamed their idiotic announcements at you, real-slow-too-just-to-get-the-p-o-i-n-t-across, you'd somehow understand them better.

Just then, Arnie and Ina pulled up to the Velvet Dragon in their Buick Regal. Arnie waved across at Dexter and shouted, "Last month it was Mexican. Now it's Chinese. Ain't had Chinese in ages!"

Dexter nodded expansively, so it could be seen from across the street. He was acting mayor and president of the Chamber of Commerce for the moment.

"Ina," he called.

Ina steadied herself with one hand on the hood and proclaimed "Spring rolls" before they vanished inside.

And now Dexter almost fell off the curb. He was looking down the block at Araceli's joint. She had changed the sign, all right. It said MOM'S COFFEE.

"What the hell is that?" Dexter cried.

"A sign," Juan explained mildly.

"That's wrong."

"No, Jefe. Is correct. A sign."

"The wording, man. The wording. It's wrong."

"No. Is one hundred percent correct. We put in apostrophe and everything."

Visser patter Juan on the shoulder.

Dexter shook his head.

Juan said, "You tell us to never write in Spanish. But you made the mistake, Jefe. You said put 'café.' Pues ya sabes — 'café' es espanish."

"No, no! 'Café' is not Spanish."

"It is."

"No it isn't."

"Is too," said Visser. "Everybody knows that."

"Oye, no mames," Juan snapped, patience about evaporated. "Is *coffee*."

"No," said Dexter. "Not in this context."

"Con qué?" said Juan.

"Lookit—'café' means restaurant."

"Guah? Are you joking me right now?"

Yoking.

"A café is a fancy li'l restaurant," Dexter explained. He huffed. He spit. "It's French or something."

Juan cursed: "Cheezits krize! French is American now?"

"Wel-l-l," sputtered Dexter, forging ahead in a manly fashion, "it's more American than Mexican."

Juan sighed.

"You people, Jefe. You no make sense." He shrugged. "We must go tell Araceli," he said.

They headed that way.

Juan noted, "You language is for locos."

"You're welcome to go back to Tollackee-packee and speak Mexican all damned day."

"Now, boys," said the rev, sipping his wine.

⁂

Araceli was unfazed by the whole crisis.

She had just heard that her sister, uncle, and nephew had made it safely to El Paso and were catching a Greyhound north. She was considering opening a liquor store.

Maybe a bar, which is where her heart was. El Farolito, she was thinking. Or El Bar No Seas Burro. Araceli was always happy. But she was done with signs.

"I can sell coffee," she said. "The sign? No big deal."

"We need food. American food. Not coffee." Dexter grabbed Visser's glass and swallowed the dregs of the wine. "Grilled cheese. Chili dogs. What I wouldn't give for a chili dog. Hell, there hasn't been a decent hot dog in this town for months."

Araceli turned her huge eyes upon him and stroked his arm.

"Pobrecito," she cooed.

She had plans for the Bower spread. As soon as she landed Old Man Dex, El Jefe. She could just imagine her new American kitchen at his place with some molcajetes and jarritos and a nice bright red ceramic crowing rooster statue and a tortilla press.

"Pobre Deysterr. Estás tan cute!"

She pinched his cheek and cracked him a cold Corona. He blushed. This is how she knew she had him hooked. She would make him fat and happy and would rub his feet.

Dexter watched her bottom work the bright blue skirt like a couple of tractor motors under a tarp. Holy smokes, that was fine, right there. He drank.

They were seated at a table. Dexter was thinking of them as The Three Amigos now—he, Juan, and Visser. Getting into the swing of things. Trying to apply the therapeutic concepts of the rev, who had given him some good sessions of the talking cure after the funeral. *Bend like a reed in the wind,* Visser had advised. *The rigid break in strong wind, Dexter. Bend like the reeds. Bend like the grasses. Weather every storm.*

Dexter was bending his ass off—like a reed, he told himself. Evergreen. Forever spring. Shit.

Araceli had created her first traditional turkey dinner. She was dying for them to sample this miraculous creation. Dexter didn't think he could eat anything at this point. He was thinking chips and nacho cheese in front of the tube in his easy chair with the fat dog snoring and farting at his feet. He eyed Visser; the pastor seemed ready to eat any number of meals in a row. Juan simply looked miserable, rubbing his head.

"Ay, mi cabeza," he said.

Visser dug around in his pocket and dropped a stone on the table. It clattered in front of Dexter. Dexter glanced down. "Arrowhead," said Visser. "Found it in my garden."

"Yeah," said Dexter. "Found a million of 'em on the farm. Used to plow 'em up all the time. Gave 'em to the boy." He sipped his beer. "He glued 'em on a board. Got it…somewhere."

Juan fingered the arrowhead.

"Wow," he said. Somehow, he turned it into Spanish. *Guau.*

Araceli delivered placemats and silverware and water to them. Then, with a flourish and a sly little wink at Dexter, she produced three plates piled with steaming turkey and deep purple beets and globs of cranberries and wads of orange sweet potatoes.

"Ah," said Dexter.

"Ajua!" said Juan.

Visser was already eating.

But Araceli wasn't done yet. She came from the kitchen bearing a Talavera pitcher that featured a primary color sun face smiling into the sad blue visage of a quarter moon. She came around the table and managed a deeply suggestive hip bump into Dexter's shoulder with her good right hip.

"Don't forget the bes' part!" she enthused.

She bent over the table and proceeded to tip the pitcher over each plate and spill a thick white goo over everything. It covered the turkey and the yams and puddled all over each plate. Roughly the texture of heavy whipping cream. Dexter couldn't, by God, tell what that was supposed to be.

"What is that?" he asked. "Gravy?"

Stung, Araceli backed away from the table and clutched the pitcher to her heart.

"Is los mash potatoes!" she cried and ran to the kitchen in humiliation. They could hear her crying in there.

Dexter rose.

"God. Damn. It," he announced. "Look here. This is my country. This is my country. We been here, working this land, forever. We made our lives here. We planted crops here. We had our children and—and we buried our loved ones here. Right here! Is it too goddamned much to ask that somebody pay the slightest fucking attention to our traditions and history and stop wrecking everything? Could you learn the language? Could you cook a simple meal that anybody from here would recognize as real food? Am I asking too much?"

He was red in the face and shaking. He was embarrassed about the whole thing—ashamed of his comment to Araceli, ashamed to have shown his emotions, ashamed that he had tears in the corners of his eyes. Outbursts were simply not the West Linden way.

Reverend Visser just stared at his own hands with his head bowed. Juan fingered the arrowhead, spun it around and around with one finger. He didn't want to eat the goopy mash potatoes either. "Yeah, Jefe. That's what Geronimo said."

Dexter stared at him. They heard Araceli blow her nose. Visser cleared his throat as if to speak, but apparently thought better of it. Juan spun the arrowhead, and Dexter wondered what tribe it had come from.

He sat back down.

He put his napkin in his lap.

He took up his fork and his knife and he bent like a reed in the wind.

"I expect you two," he said, "to eat every bite."

The rest was silence.

Twelve

Welcome to
the Water Museum

Fat orange light squatted in the brown sky. It wasn't like that every day—most days were stained-glass blue. But the dust and the smoke tended to hang there more and more. Old-timers told Billy they'd give a dollar to see a good old-fashioned gray sky full of rain. He rode his bike down County Road 120, no cars in sight. And no clouds. Somebody had painted *Droughty Road* on the signs. That was pretty funny, he thought. The corn and soybean fields were so toasted they were just dirt fields now. Billy couldn't remember the last time he'd seen a cow.

Big white wind propellers turned slowly. The kids called them sunflowers. The towers reminded Billy of those crazy alien machines from *War of the Worlds*. He really liked that one. He and his boys would fight the windmill towers with BB guns and slingshots.

The ground was crazed in crack patterns like in the westerns Pops loved, but the boys didn't like those so much.

Billy watched Pops out there in the field, standing between his pickup and the army water unit. Home from work early and working again, but as he pointed out every day—chores were never done. Pops trudged like a mule from job to job. Billy waved. Pops stood there staring at him, then waved back. At least that run of one-hundred-degree days had broken.

A trio of helicopters chugged in the distance, going from east to west. Daily rounds, checking the last crops. They looked like crows, Pops liked to say. Later in the afternoon, they'd show up on the north side of the road, flying from west to east. Going back to base.

Billy biked across the field, ramping off a couple of the crumbly old furrows. He skidded to a halt near Pops and grinned. Dust. Pops waved his hand in front of his face and coughed. He had a big plastic keg attached to the spigot at the foot of the unit.

"Thing about drought, Bill," he said, "is the air gets baked."

Billy had heard this a million times.

"Ain't just the dirt. The air gets thirsty. Sucks the water out of the dirt, the plants. And then the sun sucks it out of the air. Till there ain't no water no more."

Mom would never allow Billy to talk like Pops did. Oh no. Billy had a B+ in English, and Mom wanted him to do even better. She even tried to talk in some kind of made-up elegant way, as if anybody ever really talked like that. Not even his teachers were so phony. They had little bottles of cold water in school. The kids were always thirsty. Higgins

216

and Charlie said it was recycled pee. That grossed him out, but by about 11:00 and 2:00 every day, he didn't care and drank up.

"Way this here works," said Pops, patting the sci-fi-looking tower, "is some bunch of chemicals is all stacked up inside, in cakes. This shell is mesh, see."

"Uh-huh," he said, just to say something.

Billy looked down Route 120. Big flat sheets of land going on forever. Steel sunflowers, most of them rotating. Marching away, smaller and smaller till they blinked out in the yellow distance. He'd heard about the chemicals, too. He'd been here when the army installed them. He'd even read the manual. The Corps of Engineers guy had made it sound like they were going to have swimming pools soon with all the water from the tanks.

"And," said Pops, "the chemicals attract water through condensation. Can you spell that, Bill?"

"Sure," hoping Pops didn't give him a quiz right there.

"Idea was water in the air, free for the taking. So the chemicals suck that moisture out of the air and pass it down here through the filter and into the jug."

Billy looked into the jug. Its white plastic showed the waterline as a gray shadow. Only about two inches had accumulated.

"How long?" he asked.

Pops put his hands in his back pockets, kicked a clod. They watched it bounce away, tossing up small explosions of dust.

"A week."

"Jeez," Billy said.

"Even the air, Bill. Even the goddamned air."

Billy rolled the bike back and forth.

"The one crop a drought can't kill," Pops said, pointing to his head, "is right here."

Billy waited for the next part of the liturgy.

Pops pulled his blue bandana out of his back pocket and scrubbed his face and neck.

"Once the bees come back," he said.

"Then I'll know," Billy replied.

"That's right. That's right." Pops got in the truck. "Don't be late for supper."

"I'll know the drought is over," Billy said as the truck bumped toward home, "when the bees come back."

The dust cloud made the truck look like it was a burning fighter plane going down.

&

Chemicals, Billy thought. They'd pretty much all gone back to using outhouses because there wasn't water to flush the toilets or to bathe. The house well had long ago gone stinky and sludgy. They used it to wash dishes. The government retrofit had siphoned this "gray water" out to Mom's vegetable patch. She did all right with crunchy stuff like potatoes and carrots, but the juicy stuff like cantaloupes ended up tasting like soap. So trucks came and filled the water tanks and that was all you got for the month. The waterman always said the same thing: "It'll break soon!" And more trucks came and dumped chemicals in the out-house poo-holes—smelled like cherries. Big crazy cherry Life Savers with that dull stink beneath.

One good thing about the drought—the kids got to suck on all the hard candies they wanted. As long as they were sour candies and made their mouths water. It cut their thirst, the grown-ups said. But Billy was pretty sure he'd never eat cherry candies again.

He dropped the bike by the front steps and went in.

Mom was cooking. She mostly did microwave stuff so she wouldn't have to waste water on boiling. They ate on paper plates. She tried to make it an adventure. "Just like camping!" she liked to announce, though the kids had eaten on paper plates so long they didn't remember any-thing else.

She was kind of a dork, but Billy loved her anyway. He noticed how she took a bit of her water dose for the day and shared it with the rugrats—little Mitch and April. Pops liked to call weepy little April "April Showers." Billy wasn't able to catch all the yearning nuances in that one. He thought it was all about the tears.

"You crybaby," Billy'd say to her when she was on a ram-page about how unfair his latest Wii or Xbox bullying was.

"It's not fair!" she'd shout.

"If we bottled up all your stupid crying, we could end the drought right now!"

April would run from the room. This was the small triumph both boys enjoyed every day: making April do The Grand Exit. She had gotten so touchy, they could cause her to freak out over ever more absurd things. If they were watching TV, for example, and a hyena ate a baby zebra, all Billy had to do was say, "April, how come you didn't warn that zebra? It's totally your fault it just died!" Or, watching a UFO movie, "April, why did you just blow up the White House with your death ray?"

Her outraged shrieks and stomping journeys upstairs put a saintly smile on Billy's face.

"Kids, be nice!" Mom would holler.

Billy suspected Mom mostly took sponge baths. Judging from his scent, maybe Pops took dust baths. They kept the fans running all night. Sometimes all the dust in the atmosphere made lightning, but they never smelled rain.

⌘

"Seen a snake today," said Mitch.

"Saw," said Mom.

They were working on their chicken parm.

"Didn't see no saw," said Mitch, "saw a snake."

Pops and Billy burst out laughing.

"I swear," said Pops.

"And I saw a hammer," Billy offered.

The males all chuckled.

"Where at?" asked Pops. He was piling that cheesy

chicken into his cheek like a ground squirrel snarfing up acorns. They still had those. Squirrels, not acorns. Lived under the house.

"He was goin' under the back porch," said Mitch. He was a noodle man, mostly. Skipped the chicken. Billy called him a carbo-loader, whatever that was.

"Welp," said Pops. "There go the squirrels."

"Isn't that a shame," said Mom.

"I think that cottonwood down to the creek finally died," Pops announced.

"God, Walt," Mom said. "What next."

"I know it," he replied. "Hate to see that. But those are thirsty trees. Nothing in that creek but dirt."

Billy didn't tell them, but there were plenty of snakes down in the creek. They lived in the old beater cars and washing machines Pops had buried in the banks when there was water. In case of flash floods. Bummer about the tree, though. Billy always peed on its roots, as if he could keep it alive with his own body.

Changing the subject, Mom turned her eternally hopeful smile to Billy. It made him feel guilty. Like he could only let her down, no matter what he came up with.

"Bill? Have homework?"

"Nah."

"No, ma'am."

"…No…ma'am. Not tonight. Got that fie' morrow."

"The school called me about it toda"

Oh, no.

"They asked me to chaperone. Isn't that wonderful? Cool beans, as you might say."

Cool beans?

Bad enough they had to go to some crappy museum. But now Mom would be on the bus. So much for all the fun he was planning to have with Higgins and Charlie. So much for flirting with Samantha Rember. He called her "Sammy Remember." She scrunched her nose at him when he did.

"Cool," he said. He smiled wanly. "Beans." Thinking: *Dang it.*

The kids all excused themselves and scattered.

Pops lit his pipe, and Mom took one cold beer from the fridge and poured most of it in his glass and saved a bit for herself. They had stocked up a few cases, and they tended to be parsimonious with it. Coors. She liked the "mountain spring water" part.

She took his fingers in her hand.

"Walt...sometimes..." She shook her head and took a sip. "Lord, Lord."

He squeezed her hand.

"I know," he said. "It'll be over soon. The government's going to make rain. They do it in China, I heard. You'll see."

Mom thought about some silly thing and laughed, and did Pops, and they went to watch TV.

Before school, Billy had to help Pops adjust the solar panels. What a major pain. "You like your light and TV and computer," Pops groused, "you'll stop bitching and just help me with this goddamned panel!" Good old Pops.

His farming was on hold, but he kept busy. He was on a foundation-reaffirmation crew. Fancy words for guys who went around the state fixing drought creep: the shrinkage from dried-out soil pulling away from house foundations. There was government subsidy money in it. All those houses with cracking foundations and sloping floors from the desiccated earth pulling into itself. They hauled a slurry of cement and soil-expanding chemicals into the gaps around the houses. Everybody had to laugh because the slurry also made the basements waterproof. In his spare time, Pops installed rebuilt air-conditioning units on roofs. Insurance had started to cover that as a necessity, so business was pretty good.

Mom managed to coax enough water out of the windmill to garden an okay corn patch. Nothing like they used to, but enough for the neighbors and themselves.

She helped out at the church, too. Typing up the weekly newsletter. And she did some small jobs at the old folks' home. "Mad money," she called it. One of her terms Billy didn't get. Like when she said things were "boss." Whatever.

"All aboard!"

"Gotta go," Billy told Pops. "Mom's calling."

Pops muttered something that sounded like *Smuffle whazick*.

Billy tapped his arm and trotted away.

She drove a Windstar. It was old and nerdy and embarrassed the boys. The radio was crackly with static, and a booming voice was pontificating about how solar desalinization of seawater was a socialist plot by big government. Cheap water was a ploy by Washington to undermine the constitutional...Billy turned it off. Mom glanced at him, but said nothing.

April and Mitch went to Prairie Elementary. Mrs. G had already volunteered to take them home after school. Mom drove into the parking lot of the middle school. The Panthers sign had faded to ochre above the yellow ball field. The VISITORS scoreboard had lost letters: VIS T RS.

Bright school buses stood outside the auditorium. Billy was thinking of trying acting. The drama coach told him he'd be great in *If the Boys Wore the Skirts*.

He'd said, "You have a flair for the comedic, Billiam." What a freak! *Billiam?* WTF. Still...Could be interesting. Sammy Remember was in Drama Club. But Higgins and Charlie would never give up mocking him for wearing a dress onstage.

Mom got busy with all the boring church ladies circling around the lot, more excited than the kids. Billy piled into the back of the bus with the gang. Sammy Remember tried not to look at him. Her red hair was hot in the sun and smelled like coconuts and pineapples. Billy tried to bump into her as he passed her seat. She made him swallow when he saw her. She ignored him and attended to the weird little folding-paper game her friend Peanut was showing her. But the way the girls laughed, he just knew they were talking about him.

Sammy glanced back at him and smiled once. Blushing.

"Oh crap!" Charlie proclaimed, digging in Billy's ribs with his elbow.

Sammy and Peanut giggled, but never looked back again.

"Second base," Charlie predicted. "Today in the museum."

"For sure," Higgins agreed. "Bra. Boobs."

They had read *Playboy*.

"Knock it off," said Billy, red in the ears. "I mean, jeez."

"Billy's got a boner," Higgins said.

Billy grabbed him and they wrestled until Mom came back and said, "Do I have to separate you gentlemen?" This made Billy feel good. Sammy Remember would not forget that he was, in fact, a badass and had gotten in trouble for being too wild even before the bus pulled out. Though it was, like, a total fail that Mom was the one to scold him.

Charlie pulled a *Doctor Who* magazine out of his backpack, and the boys bent to it.

Billy popped a lemon drop in his mouth.

The sky was saffron.

"Museums suck," said Billy.

The bus rattled along between tan fields.

"Right?" said Charlie.

"History," said Higgins. "Shit like that."

"What I'm sayin'," Billy said, watching the back of Sammy's head.

"Suckage," said Charlie.

"Suckola," Higgins said.

"Sucks the big one," Billy said.

"That's what she said," Charlie said.

They all giggled like Sammy and Peanut.

The outskirts of town. Billy, in spite of himself, crowded the windows. They never saw the city for real, just in movies. Trees. Nice.

There was a car dealership. Empty. Weeds poked up through cracks they had made in the asphalt.

"Dude," said Billy. "Freakin' drought, and it's all freakin' weeds. Freakin' weeds, like, never stop growin'. Whyn't we just farm weeds?"

Higgins was asleep; Charlie was back with *Doctor Who*.

Billy rested his head against the glass and felt his mind fly out into all the windows and doors. Felt himself move in and out of the alleyways. Like a great sideways yo-yo in a dream. Like he could walk into a thousand life stories. Like he could think up a whole new world. Like he could go out of himself and keep going and find a house on a beach with ten million miles of ocean in front and sweet cold fog and afternoon rainstorms and Sammy there beside him.

This thought both comforted and stung him and made him happy and made him want to cry. How did Pops ever tell Mom he wanted to be her boyfriend? How did you do that? And—second base! Bras? How could a guy ever get up the guts to ask? How did a kiss happen, anyway?

The bus pulled into the museum parking lot and farted its air brakes and Mom stood and the doors opened.

WELCOME TO THE WESTERN PLAINS MUSEUM OF WATER.

Another sign said PILGRIM, REFRESH YOURSELF. Some kind of old covered wagon and a plaster ox out in front. Corn-ball.

The kids disembarked. Grab-ass ensued; impromptu tag, running around like idiots. "I swear," Mom said, "dealing with you all is like herding chickens."

The boys feigned disinterest in the hologram of a huge fountain in the entryway. But the girls oohed and ahhed over it—the way the fake water was projected on a cloud of steam and seemed to gush and flow and then change colors.

"Water don't turn yellow," Higgins announced.

Then the boys started snickering.

"If it does, don't drink it," Charlie said.

As an added feature, each child received a minuscule spritz of cold water in the face, and they shrieked with de-light, but were firmly denied a repeat.

They entered through a projected waterfall, a cheesy video loop playing on more steam.

Mom had once seen that effect at Disneyland on the Pirates ride.

They walked on video tiles, and each step made ripples in the fake blue water beneath them. Fat goldfish-looking things swam away from the electric ripples. The boys made big faux splashes by jumping up and down until the digital fish swam out of sight beyond the edges of the floor.

They wandered through the galleries: 3D film loops of Niagara Falls. Higgins didn't believe it.

"That crap's from the Avatar movies," he said, tossing his glasses in the big blue box.

But Billy stood as one hypnotized. He was astounded by the sight of that water. Who imagined wild water was white? And so much of it the earth used to simply throw it away. Still, he was more awed by the sound of it than the sight of it. The sheer noise.

Farther in, they witnessed seashore videos: the announcer droned, "Behold the song of the sea." The sound of crashing waves. Vents pumped saltwater scents at the kids. Gulls cried.

The moms were smiling, but the kids felt creepy, watching all this water. It felt bad. Billy picked up a conch shell and put it to his ear.

"You'll hear the sea," Mom promised.

Just sounded like the inside of a shell to him.

A friendly docent appeared in a sky-blue suit.

"You supposed to look like water?" Higgins said.

Kids laughed.

Billy looked for Sammy, caught her eye. She wasn't smiling either. She stared at him for a long time before they both looked away, blushing.

It got sucky. Charts. Data. Laser pointers.

How the drought came upon the West first, then the South, then the Midwest. Then how the water states started to flood from too much rain. The docent called this "The Cosmic Irony." And the oceans rose and the coasts were invaded by seawater. Then, how the water states instituted the border system, to keep the drought survivors from overrunning their lands. How they shipped water units to the heartland until the crisis was over. No shortage of sun or wind here, though, right, kids? So the drought states traded wind energy and solar energy to the national grid. Light for water, the government motto said. And: Light—it's the new harvest.

"How long's it been?" Billy asked.

"Pert near twenty years now," the docent said with her weird anesthetized grin.

"Seventeen," Mom said.

"Pert," Charlie snickered.

Higgins couldn't stop laughing.

"What a hick," he whispered. Then he asked, "Excuse me, miss. Were you born in 1860?" He and Charlie laughed and snorted. Billy moved away from them.

The docent ignored them.

"And now, children," she said, working a remote that caused smoked-glass doors to swing open, "we go to meet water."

They followed her through.

છ

Creepy, man. Are you kidding? What is this, Halloween? Billy's mind was racing. It was dark in there. Crazy bug noises everywhere—he wasn't used to bugs. He didn't like it. Bouncy little lights among the trees with awful gray beards hanging down.

"What's that?" he asked Mom.

"Fireflies," she said. She was *happy*. "Isn't it awesome?"

Mom trying out her kid-speak again.

"Awesome," Billy said.

He pointed.

"And what's that?"

"Spanish moss."

"Has it got spiders?"

"It's fake," said Higgins. "Dumbass."

Splashes in dark water. He squinted. *Water*. They were walking on a spit of fake ground in a big dark pool of water at night and there were freaky things croaking. Water was beneath them, looking poisonous in the gloom. Anything could be beneath it.

"What's that?" Billy asked the docent.

"What, hon?"

"That sound."

"Frogs."

One of the girls let out a tiny scream and the rest laughed.

"It jumped on me!" she cried.

"What is this place?" Billy asked.

"This would be a swamp," the docent explained. "This was the Atchafalaya basin in Louisiana before the coast deteriorated and the wetlands were destroyed. This is what you'd see."

"Are there alligators?" Mom asked.

"In the tanks, yes."

"Gators!" cried Billy. He moved closer to Mom. She put her hand on his back. It was hot and clammy. He pulled away.

Higgins snapped a girl's bra strap.

Billy heard Sammy's voice.

"Miss?" she said in the gloom. "What's wrong with the air?"

"Wrong, dear?"

"Yes, ma'am. The air feels, um, heavy or something."

"That's humidity. That's what humidity feels like."

Silence.

"I'm *glad* we're in a drought!" Charlie offered.

They moved on through a beaver dam room and an African watering hole with wack plaster elephants and a Walden Pond diorama. "Who's that dude?" Billy said, pointing to a bearded figure in front of a tiny cabin.

231

Little dragonflies hung from wires and bobbed among cattails. They stared at catfish in murky tanks. The catfish stared back. It was creepy as hell.

But the worst thing of all was The Rain Parlor.

It was a round room with concentric rings of benches with a small octagonal dais in the middle. The docent climbed up three steps and smiled down at them. "It's best if you move to the center," she said, but Billy hung back and took a bench on the outer ring. He was shaky. He felt like he had ice in his stomach. He didn't want to hear any more crap from his boys. He didn't want Mom pawing at him. He couldn't understand why she was all jazzed. He didn't like this room with its fake blue sky and its painted green fields and far little trees and its stupid little white clouds looking like sheep on the horizon. To his astonishment, Sammy Remember came and sat beside him.

They looked at each other. She smiled a little, but her face was flushed and she looked like her dog had died. She had bright pink splotches on her alabaster cheeks.

"Are you okay?" he asked.

"Oh, Billy!" she said and took his hand and put her head on his shoulder.

Whoa. Fortunately, the lights dimmed. And she started to cry—he could feel her tears soaking into his T-shirt. When it was dark enough, he put his arm around her. Then she kissed the side of his face. Followed by the horror of the rain.

~

Dark. Crickets. Then stars started to appear above them. And—what the hell was that? It looked like a scary movie. The docent's voice in the darkness: "The clouds obscure the moon." And they did—these projected huge beasts rose up and blotted out the stars and the moon, settled like a threat upon them. The clouds started flickering. "And the lightning begins."

Billy heard Mom say, "Oh!"

Bolts of light shot across the sky—much vaster and more horrifying than their little dust flashes at the farm. A bolt plunged to earth and blasted a tree apart and kicked up flames. Little speakers broadcast its crackling.

"Oh my God!" somebody yelled.

Billy heard sobbing.

When the first thunder crack boomed, they all jumped. It was so loud. It was as if God's violence had come upon them in deepest rage, dropping temples and crushing idols to the ground. Crash. And crash again. They covered their ears.

Wind started then, cold wind. The speakers made small howlings, as if electric coyotes were stalking their feet. Ghosts, perhaps. More thunder. Some kids cried as the mothers laughed and clapped.

Then came what must have been...rain.

Not real rain, of course. But the sound of it. The sizzle and the whisper and the hiss and the splash of it. The blue

233

light along the faux horizon of the room. The projected banners and veils of rain all around them. Rain like lace curtains, rain like smoke, rain like spiderwebs and flags and wind you could see. Rain that sang to their bones, that ached inside their bellies and their hands, rain that made them thirst and cower and hide. Rain they had never felt yet knew as intimately as they knew their own skins. It was dreadful. Sammy clutched Billy as hard as anyone could, and he wept into her red hair and didn't care if she knew it or not.

Higgins cried out, "Stop it, miss! Oh, stop the rain!"

But it went on and on and on, the fake electric fields filling again with the lie of freshness, springtime, life.

*

They were quiet on the way home. Billy didn't let Mom turn on the radio. The Windstar hummed along in the heat. The thermometer on the dash read 80. It was long after sunset, and the western sky had a band of red and violet spread along the edges.

Both of them had their little color picture buttons on their lapels—the docent's last ghastly blessing. Mom had a picture of an icicle. His was a moose standing in an alpine bog. She had bought a CD of frogs croaking. Billy stopped her from putting it in the CD player.

"Billy?" She said.

He turned and stared out the window.

234

"Mom," he finally said. "Is that really the way the world used to be?"

She glanced at him.

"Crickets," he said. "Frogs. Clouds. Like that?"

She sighed.

"Yes, honey. Just like that."

Five more miles.

"All that color." He shuddered a little. "All that noise."

"Son?"

"So cold, Mom."

He shook his head, watching his own reflection in the window.

"But wasn't the museum wonderful?" she said.

Sammy. That word kept turning in his head. The scent of coconut red hair. The dry lip-pop on his cheek that in future years would remind him of a pigeon pecking at a grain of bread, but which now contained all hope and fear and desire and a vivid dreamed future expanding forever inside his body. He almost told her he loved her. The way her eyes lit up under the lightning.

"Mom?" he said.

"Billy?"

"How do you ask a girl for a kiss?"

She stifled a small laugh.

"Oh, my," she said. "Well, I think you know when the time is right. Then you just do it."

"How do you know?"

"It's like the rain. You just know it's coming."

They drove on.

"Mom?"

"Yes?"

"Do me a favor?"

"Of course."

"Please," he said. "Please. Don't ever take me to that place again."

"Why, Billy?"

He bent over and put his arms over his head and did not look up.

Mom drove on in silence, remembering how, when she was a girl, she had run along the banks of the Missouri River. It surged and sang as if water could never run out. It was summer vacation. She kissed her first boy there. The water, the water, she felt it running through her body still. She could hear it. And she rode that beautiful tide, wind lifting her hair, trying to tell him about the copper sea.

Thirteen

Bid Farewell to Her Many Horses

The Indians weren't talking to me. At Gabe's food store, they looked away when I bought a soda. There were three of them in there, plus Gabe's wife. Just to tweak them, I popped the lid right there and chugged it. Obviously, word had gotten around the res. They knew why I'd come, but they didn't know what to think of it. I felt bad enough. Their anger only made it worse.

Out in the light, I felt eyes watching me. The perfect smell of South Dakota was all over the street—I could fly in that air, fat with miles of prairie and storm clouds rushing from Nebraska to Iowa. I hunched up my shoulders. White boys visiting Pine Ridge can't help but remember all those cowboy movies. You listen for a whistling arrow, prepare for the mortal *thwack* when the shaft nails you between the shoulder blades. Well, at least this white boy does. I probably had it coming.

I'd married one of the local girls. Her family didn't want her to marry me. They didn't want her to marry a white guy, but we were wild for each other. We ran off to Dead-

239

wood, to a small chapel near the casinos. The minister was a Brulé Sioux. She was Oglala. We took our honeymoon in the Black Hills—Paha Sapa, she told me, the center of the world. We stayed in a small hotel below Mount Rushmore. We bought those T-shirts that show four huge bare asses and say: *Rear View Mt. Rushmore*. We laughed. Everything was funny.

Then the usual tough years. We went to California, both of us trying college. She tried writing to her family, but they were fighting mad. Our few visits back to the reservation were grim. I thought I was lonesome, but what happened to her heart out in California was a terror to see. I'd catch her staring up at the rattling palm trees sometimes, this look of sorrow on her face that almost seemed like rapture.

And she couldn't get out of the bottle. They blamed me. I started to believe it, too. I'd fooled her away from people, her world. Empty bottles, hidden at first beneath the sink, behind the apartment, clanked in the trash basket. She was quiet, as old-time Indian women are, and she wore a long braid in the old way. When she crashed the car, they say the braid was caught in the glass of the window. I don't know—I couldn't bear to look at the body. I sent her home on a train. It took me two days to drive out after her, and now I was burying my wife in the little graveyard near Our Lady of the Sioux. The headstone was already made. It said: JONI HER MANY HORSES. DAUGHTER, SISTER. WE WILL MISS YOU. 1960–1990. They left my name off entirely.

Don Her Many Horses was Joni's oldest brother. Back in high school, when our teams played the Indians from Red Cloud, Don was a monster on the basketball courts. The way things were in those days, though, Indian boys didn't get too many victories. Even when they won. It was easy—the refs called them foul, or ejected them from the games for the least infraction. If they did win, they'd get their asses kicked after the game if we could find them ... if there were more of us than them.

I made the mistake once of cracking wise to Don on the court. After one spectacular drive to the basket—when Don seemed to be floating over our heads for an impossible distance, then drove the ball down through the hoop so it caught no net, just streaked and hit the floor like a rock—I sidled up to him. I did what all us whites did in those days, dreaming of ourselves in Technicolor cowboy hats, our ideas as fixed as Mount Rushmore, made sick in our hearts whenever we saw an Indian smile, certain somehow his smile took something away from our own souls.

"Hey, Chief," I said. "You got-um heap good medicine, huh? Y—"

Bang.

I was gone from the world.

When I came to in the shower room, it was like drifting out of deep purple water flecked with chips of fire. They brushed my skin as I surfaced. A million sweaty

241

and hysterical dudes were glaring down at me. "Bobby!" they were shouting. "Bobby!" Don Her Many Horses was in jail, charged with aggravated assault. There had been trouble with the Indian kids, both teams slugging it out on the court. Cops had come in, sticks swinging. I listened to them babbling all about it as I stood in the shower, letting the water claw into my back and scalp. My left eye was tender as cube steak, and I could tell it was turning black.

"Shit," I said to no one in particular, "that brave sure can pack a punch!"

We all laughed and said the standard anti-Indian things you say. But I knew I was wrong. Here Don had made a spectacular play and I had gone and opened my big ignorant mouth. I don't know that it changed my life. Maybe a little bit. I didn't turn all religious or anything over it.

Don Her Many Horses wasn't much interested in me at that point. He was slumped on the cot in his cell, nursing a collection of welts and eggs coming up all over his forehead. He had a rusty-bloody old rag soaked from the tin sink and held over one eye. I watched the water drops fall and hit the knee of his jeans. They shone bright for a second, then sank in, spreading a color like grape juice as the denim darkened.

"Hi," I said.

"Fuck you, Bobby."

I ducked my head.

"Listen," I said. "I want to apologize for what happened."

He looked up at me. That eye was about swollen shut.

"Apologize, huh?" he said. He smiled a little. "All right. Go ahead."

"Sorry."

He stared at me with his one black eye. He didn't talk. That's one thing that drives you crazy with the Indians. Sometimes they just don't say anything. You don't know if they are thinking or laughing at you or what.

"I'm ...," I said, "sorry. You know. About that wisecrack. And now you're in jail."

"Yeah, I can see that," he said.

Another pause.

"You got any chew?" he said.

I dug my tin of Copenhagen out of my back pocket and tossed it to him. Those boys, when they're not smoking, they're chewing. The women, too. Joni always had a little plug of peppermint tobacco pinched into her lip. I gave it up after high school. Don does it to this day.

I was thinking about leaving when he spoke. "You know what?" he said. "Next time I see you, I might have to take me a scalp. I might skin you, too. Brain-tan your hide and have me a new pelt to paint my winter count on. Hang your balls from my war lance. 'Course, everybody'd have to get up *real close* to see 'em."

There was nothing to say to that, so I left. I could hear

his back-of-the-throat little laugh skittering around behind
me as I walked down the hall. Damned Indians.

ধ

The reservation medical examiner was taking care of Joni.
I couldn't even look at the building as I drove by. I hooked
south, out of Pine Ridge village, heading toward White
Clay, Nebraska. A couple of the guys driving around recognized me. Yellowhorse waved, one of the Red Clouds
nodded imperiously at me, raising one hand as he coasted
by in his old Ford pickup. They were burning a small pile of
tires outside of town; the smoke rose like a mourning veil
torn by wind. It angled away, fading to a haze that reached
all the way out to the edge of the Badlands. The grass
looked like Marilyn Monroe's hair. Horses swept through it
like combs.

   I was listening to KILI, "The Voice of the Lakota Na-
tion." They were playing a twenty-megaton dirge by Metal-
lica. It was followed by some Sioux music—The Porcupine
Singers. If I listened long enough, they'd probably toss in
some jazz and three Johnny Cash songs. There were supposed to be announcements of Joni's burial on there, but I
never did hear any. I pulled up at the gate of the Her Many
Horses spread. Don was walking a mottled gray horse in
slow circles in front of their house. He ran his hand along
the horse's flank; its skin jumped at his touch. It was limping. He glanced up at me and turned back to the horse.

I dropped the section of barbed wire fence that served as a gate and drove through.

"Close the gate!" Don hollered.

"I know, I know," I muttered to myself. Six dogs and four young horses headed for the opening, but I beat them to it. The horses veered away, suddenly innocent and fascinated by the sage plants beside the drive. The dogs charged me, then collapsed in the dirt, wagging their tails.

I drove up to Don, shut off the engine, and got out.

"She's sick," he said.

The old horse looked like rain clouds. I recognized her. They called her Stormy. "That's Joni's old horse," I said.

Stormy put her giant old face next to Don's. He rubbed her long white upper lip. "That's okay," he murmured. "That's okay now."

"I'm sorry, Don," I said. "I did my best."

"Stormy's dyin'," he said. He had this disconcerting way of ignoring what I said. "I've been feeding her this medicine they give me down in Rapid. But them vets don't know shit about horses. You know it? She's got these tumors."

He stroked Stormy's side. I saw that she was bloated, her abdomen distended like a barrel behind her ribs. "Now we got to kill her."

Stormy snorted.

"Go on now," he said to her. "Go ahead." She limped away.

"Them mother-effers."

"Don?" I said. "I'm sorry about Joni. I mean, I'm sorry about Stormy, too. But what I mean..."

One of the dogs nosed my crotch.

"Stop it," said Don. "I got a trailer pulled around back. You sleep there. Got food if you're hungry."

He lit a cigarette and walked away.

⌀

Night on the reservation is like night nowhere else. They say flying saucers visit the Sioux lands. Flying saucers and ghosts. When you're out there, there's a blackness that's deeper than black. The stars look like spilled sugar. You can hear the grass sometimes like water. Like somebody whispering. And the weird sounds of the night animals. Anything could happen. You get scared, and it's for a reason that hides behind the other reasons—behind the silence, and the coyotes, and the dogs barking, and the eerie voice of the owl. It's that *this is not your land. This is their land. And you don't belong.* A thousand slaughtered warriors ride around your camp, and you think it's the breeze. And they wonder why you're there.

I had the sleeping bag pulled over my head. It smelled like dust. My wife was lying five miles away, her breasts already dense as leather in death, her eyelashes intertwined, the perfect brown tunnels of her eyes sealed, the path within already forgotten. "Joni," I said. "Joni. Joni."

♂♀

I met her at night. Off the reservation, there are small joints scattered all along the roads. You can go in there for ice cream or burgers or beer. Lots of them sell Indian art and beads to the tourists, and a bunch of them still won't let an Indian in the door. The reservation folks knew which stores wanted them and which didn't.

We were in one that didn't. Six of the footballers from our school were in there with me. It was one of those dull nights. Red Cloud School had won the football game. They'd all been going down to see that *Little Big Man* movie, and they were all turned on. They were crazy-wild. Nobody could catch them.

Franklin Standing Bear's car broke down. He came walking up to the place from the road to Hot Springs. I watched him through the window, materializing out of the blackness. He paused in the parking lot, looking at us. His glasses glittered in the lights. I nudged one of the boys and pointed with my chin.

"Gaw-damn," he said.

We left our spoons sinking into our sundaes and gawked.

Franklin came in the door and ducked his head.

"More balls 'n brains," one of the football boys said.

Franklin went to the register and asked to use the phone. Sonny, the owner, had served in Korea with Franklin's dad, so he let him on the phone. But he told him he'd best get moving as soon as he was through.

We hustled out to the lot and waited for him, all jittery with crazy heat.

Franklin came out and our quarterback called, "Hey, boy!"

He put his hands up in front of him and said, "Not looking for trouble."

"You calling me a troublemaker?" the footballer asked.

"Look," Franklin said, "My car's busted down. That's all."

"You Indian boys did pretty good tonight," said the tight end. He looked like a chimp in the half light. All beady glittery eyes, stupid with lust. Jeez, this is how it begins, I thought.

"I don't know nothing about it," said Franklin, "I was over to Rosebud." He was drifting away.

"Rosebud," the first footballer said. "What kind of a faggot name is that, Standing Bear? You Indians all faggots or what? That why you got them ponytails?"

Franklin had a frozen smile on his face. He could see a freight train coming and he couldn't get out of its way.

"Let's go inside," I said. I tugged on the tight end's sleeve. "C'mon," I said.

Franklin Standing Bear spit on the ground.

"You know what?" he said. "You're just a bunch of lowlife shit-lipped pud-pulling cow fuckers. I'm about fed up with your bullshit, so come on cowboys! Fuck it! *Hoka hey!*"

Oh man, I thought, he's doing his war cry. It was a good day to die. Franklin was in full-on warrior mode now.

The footballer grunted and charged at him. Franklin leaped about three feet high and kicked him precisely in the mouth. Franklin's glasses flew one way; blood and teeth flew the other. The footballer fell back, squealing, rolling on the blacktop with his fingers in his mouth. They closed in on Franklin, but he broke for the road. All our boot heels sounded like three horses crossing a highway. I didn't know what the hell I was doing. I was just running.

Two sets of headlights rounded the curve, and Franklin dodged between them. Indians poured out at us, like they were flying out of the light. One of them was Joni. She cornered me, waving a tire iron in my face. God, she was beautiful. She looked like a wolf—her small perfect teeth were bared, the muscles in her arms tight with rage. She was wearing a small choker. The cold had made her nipples stand up. She hissed and cussed at me. In her cowboy boots, she was taller than I was. I was sure she was going to knock my head loose. The sound of massacre was all around us. Don appeared beside Joni, grinning. He was panting from the fighting, flushed and sweaty.

"Well, well," he said. "It's the Indian lover." He turned to Joni. "This here is a big Indian lover. Isn't that right, Bobby?"

Joni stopped waving the iron at me.

"Hey," said Don. "You come out here to *apologize?*"

There was a scattered rubble of white boys all over the road.

"I don't know," I said.

"You don't know," Joni taunted.

"I don't know." I was looking around.

"Looks like you picked the wrong place to be," she said. "That's for damn sure."

But they didn't do anything about it. We walked over to Don's car—a ferocious orange Chevy Impala—and Don drove us back to the side of the lot and put me out. "Forgive us," he said in the phoniest arch-sounding accent, "if we shan't stop in for tea." They burned rubber. They were doing those manic *yip-yip* war cries as they sped away. I thought Joni waved good-bye, but I couldn't be sure.

We met again at a movie theater, by accident. I finally got down to see *Little Big Man,* and damned if I didn't wish I was a Sioux warrior. Somebody in the balcony kept pelting me with popcorn, though, but every time I turned around, there was nobody there. I finally jumped out of my seat and glared up there. Joni was laughing down at me. I blushed. After that, I kept thinking of that massacre at the Indian village—I kept thinking of a soldier shooting Joni in the back as she ran. It made me sick inside. I couldn't get the picture out of my mind. I was Dustin Hoffman, and I watched Joni run and die, run and die, in slow motion, extreme close-up. The next time we saw each other, we were on.

♉

Morning. Horses. They walked in patient circles around the trailer, snorting as they went past the screened window,

trying to get a whiff of me without letting me know they
were inspecting. Today was the burial. I got up, dragged on
my jeans and a T-shirt, and stepped out. They trotted away
with their ears bent back and their tails lifted. I went in the
house quietly, but Don was already up, sitting at the table
drinking coffee. He gestured to a skillet with three eggs and
some bacon fried up. "Toast," he said, nodding to a stack of
bread slices on a saucer before him. Silent, I got my breakfast and sat across from him. We stared at each other as I
ate. Don's boy, Snake, was asleep on the couch, facedown.
Elinore Her Many Horses could be heard taking a shower.
I was through eating. "Thanks," I said. "Put them dishes in
the sink, hey?" he said. I did it. Then I waited my turn for
the shower. Then it was time to go. I drove in my truck
alone.

Between breakfast and packing to leave, I can't remember
the day. As soon as I saw the coffin, it hit me in the ribs,
like a shovel swung by a batter. I kept focusing on breathing, dragging in air and letting it out slowly. My memory
of everything else is a vague gray hum. I know that one
of the Catholic Brothers from Red Cloud School led the
service, and somebody played piano. I can't remember anybody's face, just the thought: *breathe-breathe-breathe*. Then
we were standing on the steps of the church like a real family, and I shook hands with a faceless crowd. I didn't cry.

At the graveyard, I stood behind Don, about three paces, and watched the grass waver in the breeze. And afterward, I stopped at Red Cloud's grave to pay my respects to the old chief. Some Oglalas had left him tobacco ties, little sacred bundles in all the colors of the four directions. I asked him to take care of my woman out there, where she was new and maybe lost. I asked him to take her into his lodge and protect her until I could come for her. That's all I remember.

I rolled Don's sleeping bag carefully, taking pains to leave the little trailer neat. It was already late afternoon. We'd sat around inside, sipping coffee, murmuring. The television was on, turned down low. Snake stared at MTV, never looking up. Elinore sat beside me on the couch, and she periodically got up and fed me cookies or more coffee, though I didn't ask for any. After tending to the sleeping bag, I stuffed my jeans into a small duffel, and stepped outside and headed across Don's pasture, away from the trailers to the dark hump of the sweat lodge he'd built near a small stand of cottonwoods. I walked down to the stream that cuts through Don's eighty acres. There was one spot, one small white gravel pool where Joni and I made love.

It was perfectly matched to my memory, like a photo pinned inside my skull. I remembered every detail, even the giggling terror that Don, or their old man, Wilmer, would catch us at it. I stood there watching the wasps sip water at the edge of the pool, where the gravel gave way to mud. I half-expected to see the double-seashell imprint of her bottom on the shore. Dragonflies tapped the water. I'd moved in her, minnows between our legs, tickling us. Bubbles came out of her body and ran over my sides.

There were tiny smears of black hair in her armpits. Her nipples were small and dark as nuts. She hardly had any hair on her body. Afterwards, as we lounged in the water, chewing leaves of spearmint that grew on the banks, she played with the hair on my chest. She scratched it; I could hear her nails scraping. I leaned up on one elbow, watching my seed rise from her and drift. It looked like a pearl column of smoke.

"Bobby."

I jumped. I looked around, feeling caught.

It was Don. He had a rifle on one shoulder. He was leading Stormy. They were dark against the sky. Huge.

"I ...," I said. "I guess I saw a ghost."

Don nodded.

Stormy brushed flies away from her sides with lazy smacks of her tail.

"Wanna come?" he said, gesturing to the horse with his head.

I clambered up the bank and followed him. You could hear bees working the alfalfa and the sweetgrass. Stormy's limping gait played on the ground like a drumbeat. Don stared at the ground as we walked. She wheezed, the sound pitifully hollow and weak.

"Stormy thinks we're having fun," he said.

Her ears still turned to each sound. She watched a dove burst out of a small bush and fly away. She dipped her head at tall grasses, though she couldn't eat anymore. I noticed her legs trembling.

We took her over a small hillock, out of sight of the house and the other horses. "All right now," Don murmured. He eased the bit out of her mouth and pulled off the bridle. She worked her long yellow-brown teeth. She stared off.

Don cranked a round into the chamber. The lever sounded cool and final as it slid home.

"I tried," I said. He didn't look at me. "Whatever I did wrong, I loved your sister."

Don petted Stormy.

"I know it," he said. "Shit. I guess we all know it."

He raised the gun and fired into her head, behind her left ear. It was a sharp little *crack*, like a dry branch snapping. I jumped. She jerked her head straight up and fell. Her legs just vanished. Don had to dance out of her way when she dropped. The whole thing was unbelievable, some kind of trick. One of her hooves twitched, she groaned; then it was done. The silence was like a curtain in a play. You couldn't even see any blood. Don was standing there, the smoking rifle loose in his grip. I looked up at him—his eyes were closed, his head went back, and he began to sing.

He began to sing, quietly at first, but it grew louder as he went. Long, mysterious Sioux sounds, Indian words that could have been going out to God, or to Stormy, or to Joni, there was no way of knowing. But his voice rose, became a haunted sound, a cry from someplace else. I wanted to join him. I wanted to sing, to cry my pain and loss to Him—to the Grandfather, to the one she'd called *Wakan Tanka*. But I had no song, I had no prayer. I felt so small beside the voice of Don Her Many Horses.

I closed my eyes and stood with him. The good horse smell still rose from Stormy. And he sang. I started to sob, it just tore out of me. I thought I might fall down, but his hand gripped my upper arm to steady me. The wind sighed around us, and there were crows. Don kept singing, but he had slowed, enunciating carefully, and I realized he wanted me to follow. My voice was weak at first, tentative, but I repeated the sounds. He waited until I grew strong in my song.

We sang for a long time, together. We sang until dark. We sang until I thought we would never find our way home.

Acknowledgments and Credits

My first reader is always my Cinderella. Thank you to Julie Barer, agent extraordinaire. And to Michael Cendejas at the Pleshette Agency, my movie man. And to Trinity and Kevin at The Tuesday Agency—you keep me on the road and before the public.

Some of these works first appeared in *Six Kinds of Sky*, published by Cinco Puntos Press in El Paso—thanks and love to Bobby and Lee Byrd. "Mr. Mendoza's Paintbrush" was made into a stunning graphic novel from the same publishers; it was drawn by Christopher Cardinale. A couple of these tales appeared in *Orion*—thanks, Jennifer Sahn and Chip Blake. And a couple more appeared in the Akashic *Noir* series. Thanks, Johnny Temple and honorable editors. Somehow, "Amapola" won the Edgar Award. And "Bid Farewell..." was fortunate to have varied incarnations on NPR's *Selected Shorts* series.

Thank you to Reagan Arthur and everyone at Little, Brown.

Special thanks to Geoff Shandler.

Acknowledgments and Credits

PUBLICATION CREDITS:

"Amapola" appeared in *Phoenix Noir*;

"Bid Farewell to Her Many Horses" appeared in *Blue Mesa Review* (thanks to Rudolfo Anaya);

"Chametla" appeared in *Tin House* (thanks to Rob Spillman);

"Mr. Mendoza's Paintbrush" appeared in *Six Kinds of Sky*;

"Mountains Without Number" appeared in *Orion*;

"The National City Reparation Society" appeared in *San Diego Noir*;

"The Sous Chefs of Iogüa" appears here for the first time;

"The Southside Raza Image Federation Corps of Discovery" appeared in *Orion*;

"Taped to the Sky" appeared in *Six Kinds of Sky*;

"A Visit to the Water Museum" appears here for the first time;

"The White Girl" appeared in *Latinos in Lotusland* (thanks to Dan Olivas);

"Young Man's Blues" appeared in the *Esquire* anthology *You and Me and the Devil Makes Three*.

About the Author

A finalist for the Pulitzer Prize, Luis Alberto Urrea is the bestselling author of *The Devil's Highway*, *The Hummingbird's Daughter*, *Into the Beautiful North*, and *Queen of America*, among others. He has won the Lannan Literary Award, the Pacific Rim Kiriyama Prize, an American Book Award, the Christopher Award, and an Edgar Award, among other honors. Born in Tijuana to a Mexican father and an American mother, he lives outside of Chicago and is a distinguished professor of creative writing at the University of Illinois–Chicago.